"Oh, Paige. You were meant to wear that gown," Corinne said, holding her hand to her chest. She was standing behind Paige, but Paige could see her in several of the mirrors. Pain and regret filled Corinne's eyes as she looked Paige up and down and forced a smile.

Paige's heart went out to Corinne, and she turned to face her for real. The skirts swished around her as she moved, then settled like light little clouds around her feet.

"Are you sure you want to be here?" Paige asked softly. "I know if my man were marrying some-one else, I would want to be as far away from the proceedings as possible."

"No, I think this is good for me," Corinne said, taking a deep breath and lifting her chin. "The more I'm here, the easier it'll be for me to accept that this is really happening, that I'm really going to have to give him up."

Corinne's voice cracked slightly on her last words, but she managed a smile.

Paige nodded, impressed with Corinne's brav-ery, but inside she felt sick to her stomach. If love could cause a person this much pain, maybe it wasn't all it was cracked up to be.

THE QUEEN'S
CURSE

Charmed®

Published by Simon & Schuster

THE QUEEN'S CURSE

An original novel by Emma Harrison

Based on the hit TV series created by

Constance M. Burge

SIMON SPOTLIGHT ENTERTAINMENT
New York   London   Toronto   Sydney

S|S|E

SIMON SPOTLIGHT ENTERTAINMENT
An imprint of Simon & Schuster Children's Publishing Division
1230 Avenue of the Americas, New York, New York 10020
® & © 2005 Spelling Television Inc. All Rights Reserved.
All rights reserved, including the right of reproduction in whole or in part in any form.
SIMON SPOTLIGHT ENTERTAINMENT and related logo are trademarks of Simon & Schuster, Inc.
Manufactured in the United States of America
First Edition 10 9 8 7 6 5 4 3 2 1
Library of Congress Control Number 2004117777
ISBN 1-4169-0024-1

THE QUEEN'S
CURSE

Chapter One

"How did my life end up like this?" Paige Matthews asked aloud. There was no one around to answer her unless one of the many pedestrians on the busy San Francisco sidewalk wanted to venture a guess, but the question needed to be asked. "I was a social worker. I was helping people on a daily basis. People who *needed* my help. I did not go to college for four years so that I could lug around boxes of Ping-Pong balls."

It wasn't as if Paige was struggling under the weight of the box. Ping-Pong balls, after all, were mostly air. The problem was the sheer width and height of the package. It was about three feet long and three feet high, and with her small frame and slight armspan, she could barely see over the thing, and her fingers were strained from clutching the sides. And on a bright and sunny day like this one, every shopper, jogger, and mother with a baby carriage was out on the streets to act as obstacles for her to dodge blindly.

Plus, she really shouldn't have worn her new three-inch stacked-heel sandals. They were not the most comfortable shoes on the planet, nor were they great for balance, but they matched her lime green sundress so perfectly. . . .

"There has to be something better out there for me," Paige muttered to herself, placing the box down on the back of a bus stop bench. She balanced it with one hand and adjusted the thong on her sandal with the other. Wincing in pain, she looked down at her toes and saw an angry red blister forming. Great. Just what she needed.

"Hey, lady! You always talk to yourself?" a burly guy in a leather jacket asked, sneering at her as he strolled by.

"Ha-ha. Move it along, buddy," Paige said, rolling her eyes at him.

The guy snorted a laugh and kept walking. Paige glared after him. A real gentleman would have offered to help her with the box instead of laughing at her. Of course, if Paige knew anything, it was that there was a serious shortage of real gentlemen in today's world. Her brother-in-law, Leo, was one obvious exception, but he hardly counted since he was the product of a whole other generation. Nope. When it came to guys born and raised in the late twentieth century, Paige had not met a decent one for a good long time. These days, she was considering giving up on love altogether.

Paige sighed and looked up the street toward the alleyway between Chung's Chinese Cuisine and The Gap. All she had to do was get to that alley and then up the three flights of stairs to Artemis Marcus's apartment and she would be fine. Artemis was the so-called artist Paige was currently temping for. Half an hour ago he had received a call from the sporting goods shop in his neighborhood to let him know his Ping-Pong balls were in, and he had sent Paige out to fetch them. What he needed the balls for, she had no idea, but considering he had made his last sculpture entirely out of candy bar wrappers, she figured it was pointless to ask. Besides, over the past week Paige had learned that Artemis did not like to be questioned. He threw monster hissy fits, in fact, almost every time she opened her mouth.

Better get these balls back to him before he has an aneurysm, Paige thought, hoisting the awkward box again. *Or maybe he's supposed to have an aneurysm. Maybe that's why I'm here.*

Paige was the youngest of the Charmed Ones—three sisters who were the most powerful witches of all time. Together with her eldest sister, Piper, and middle sister, Phoebe, Paige fought the powers of darkness on a daily basis. Little did she know that when she quit her day job and started temping, she would keep stumbling onto more and more supernatural quandaries.

She had been going out on temp jobs for the past few months, and with every new post came another magical problem. Paige had been able to use her witchy powers to help almost every person she had worked for, or at least to help one of their employees. It was like fate was intervening to send Paige on jobs where people didn't just need someone to answer the phones—where they, coincidentally, needed a Charmed One's specific talents as well.

But Paige just could not figure out what Artemis could possibly need from her. He was nothing but an overprivileged brat, living off Mummy and Daddy's money, making bad art and whining about how no one appreciated him in his time. What on earth had the Powers That Be sent her here to do?

Shifting the box slightly to the side, Paige looked down to navigate the seam between the concrete sidewalk and the brick-floored alleyway. Just as she took her first step, a group of teenage girls came careening out of a boutique. Their bags flying, their cell phones trilling, they gabbed and laughed as they strutted along. Paige opened her mouth to shout a warning as they barreled toward her, blind to the world outside their own little bubble, but she was too late. One of the girls' shoulders slammed into the side of the box. Paige stumbled backward, caught her heel in the groove between two of the bricks, and lost her grip on the box. She made a grab for it, but it was already out of reach, tipping forward, spewing Ping-Pong balls out in every direction. A last-ditch grope for balance failed and Paige went down, scraping her bare leg on the concrete. She gritted her teeth against the pain, as right before her eyes a thousand Ping-Pong balls bounced all along the alleyway.

Why, oh why, was I not born with Piper's power? Paige lamented inwardly. The whole freezing time thing would have come in mighty handy just then.

"Oops. Sorry," the linebacker girl said, laughing into her hand along with her friends as they all scurried away.

"Yeah. Whatever," Paige said under her breath. It took all of her willpower to keep from giving up and orbing home to a nice warm bath.

Just as she pressed her hands into the ground to stand up, a pair of battered black boots appeared in her line of vision.

"Allow me," a voice said. A deep, sexy, male voice. Someone grabbed her elbows lightly and hoisted her to her feet with no effort, as if she were as light as a feather.

Normally, Paige wasn't big on strangers touching her, but something about this man's hands kept her from pulling away. They were gentle and strong, almost comforting, as if he were someone she had known her entire life.

"Are you hurt?" the man asked.

Paige blinked and looked up at him for the

first time. Her heart stopped for a split second, then slammed into her rib cage, then started pounding so fast it felt like she was sprinting toward a finish line. She was gazing into the warmest, deepest pair of chocolate brown eyes she had ever seen. They were so amazing she couldn't tear her gaze away . . . until he smiled a perfect, kind, lopsided smile. Then she couldn't stop staring at his mouth.

"Did you hit your head?" he asked.

Somewhere in the depths of Paige's mind she realized she was being spoken to. *Say something!* a little voice within her squealed. *Say something or he's going to think you're an escaped lunatic!*

Paige slowly shook her head. This was not like her. She did not get stunned speechless by men. "I . . . uh . . . no," she said. "I'm fine. Thanks."

"Good," he said, finally releasing her arms.

Paige instantly missed the warmth of his skin and wrapped her arms around herself to keep from shivering. What had gotten into her?

Snap out of it! He's just a guy! she told herself, defying her rapidly beating heart. *What are the chances he's different from the one hundred and one other losers you've met in your life?*

"So . . . are you training for the Olympic table tennis team or something?" he asked, turning toward the alley.

"No, nothing that noble," Paige said.

She glanced down at his perfectly broken-in

jeans. He was wearing a black T-shirt, and he had some kind of cool symbol tattooed on his bicep in basic black. His blond hair had that "I care enough, but not too much" tousle. Where had this guy *come* from? The Land of the Perfect?

"Well, let me help you clean this up," he said, crouching down to right the cardboard box.

"No. That's okay," Paige said, kneeling next to him and grabbing up a couple of the Ping-Pong balls. "You've probably got things to do . . . places to be. . . ." *A girlfriend to see*, she added silently. Because that would be just her luck.

She brought her hand down on the lip of the box to steady herself, and her pinkie finger brushed his. The minute contact sent such a sizzle of warmth through Paige's skin that for a second she thought a lightning storm was moving in. Her eyes met his and she knew, she just *knew* he had felt it too.

"I'm Colin," he said, holding out his hand.

Paige looked at his fingers a long moment. She wasn't sure her body could handle that much contact with his. But it would be rude to ignore him.

"Paige," she said, grasping his hand. She had to hold her breath against the crashing wave of attraction that hit her.

Suddenly, Colin was hoisting her to her feet again. Paige's pulse was pounding in her ears so loudly she could barely hear the traffic on the street less than fifteen feet away. She had never felt anything like this before. Not when she first met a guy. Could this possibly be the mythical love at first sight she was always hearing about?

"So, what's with all the Ping-Pong balls, really?" Colin asked. "You've gotta tell me or I'm going to be thinking about it all day."

I kind of like the idea of you thinking about me all day, Paige thought. "I'm working for an artist, and he's using Ping-Pong balls in his latest project," she said, looking around at the alley floor. "At least he *thinks* he is."

Colin laughed. "Well, that sounds . . . interesting."

"It's really not," Paige said. "In fact it's one hundred percent the opposite of interesting."

"Well, my guess is you make it interesting," Colin said.

Paige flushed and smiled. "Nice line."

"It's not a line," he said earnestly, taking an infinitesimal step closer to her. "Listen, I don't normally do this, but . . . do you think I could call you sometime . . . Paige?" Colin asked.

Wow. "Absolutely," Paige said breathlessly.

"Good," Colin said, showing that killer smile again. "Because I really want to hear how this whole Ping-Pong ball thing turns out for you."

Paige smiled, her eyes lingering on his. This was going to be something big—she could feel it. Somehow she managed to tear her gaze away, dig into her bag, and pull out a pen and an old scrap of paper. She scrawled her number on it and pressed it into his palm.

"I don't normally do this either," Paige said. "So don't disappoint me."

There. That sounded more like her. She was even managing to flirt a little! Colin grinned and lifted her hand toward his mouth.

"I won't." He pressed his lips against her skin and smiled. "Good luck," he said. Then he took one lingering step back, turned, and disappeared around the corner.

Paige let out a breath and leaned back against the cool wall of the alley. Her chest was heaving up and down and her legs actually felt weak. How was it possible that someone could have such a profound effect on her in the space of five minutes? But already she couldn't wait to see him again, was practically salivating for it. What could this possibly be but love?

And I was just thinking that there are no gentlemen left in the world, Paige thought, pushing herself away from the wall. She paused, a thought hitting her hard. Maybe *this* was why fate had sent her on this job. Maybe she was supposed to meet Colin. Perhaps they wanted to reward her for all her good deeds, and her prize was a date with the most perfect man on earth.

Paige glanced down the alleyway and surveyed the damage. The grime-covered ground was dotted with hundreds of tiny white balls,

some having bounced all the way to the overflowing Dumpster at the far end of the bricks. It
would take her hours on her hands and knees to
gather all of them up and put them back where
they belonged. Paige knew she shouldn't do it,
but she was feeling kind of high on life and dar-
ing after her meeting with Colin. She checked
behind her to make sure no one was watching,
then lifted her hand and spoke.

"Balls," she said.

Suddenly, a million dots of white light
swirled all over the alleyway, and Ping-Pong
balls flew off the ground from every direction,
gathering into a big white blob in the air. Paige
flicked her hand toward the open box and the
white orbs disappeared, leaving the Ping-Pong
balls safely back in their package.

All in a moment's work.

Just then a window high above her head
slammed open and Paige jumped.

"Yo! Patricia! I'm not paying you to stand
around!" Artemis shouted down from his studio.

Paige's heart skipped a beat, knowing how
close she had just come to being caught in the act
of magic. She had known Colin for only five seconds and already she was throwing caution to
the wind. Not good.

"The name's Paige," she said under her
breath, redirecting her self-irritation at Artemis.

Paige grabbed the box and tottered over to

the side door of the apartment building. If she and Colin became a couple, she would just have to remember to be more careful in the future. Paige giggled giddily at the thought of her and Colin together as she backed through the door. She was getting *way* ahead of herself, but there was nothing wrong with a little daydreaming. Suddenly there was a whole new kind of magic in the air.

"I don't think I've ever eaten so much in my life," Paige said, laying a hand over her stomach as she and Colin climbed the steps in front of Halliwell Manor the following night.

"Same here," Colin said. "I had heard that restaurant was good, but not—"

"Not 'feed me till I burst' good?" Paige joked.

"Exactly," Colin said with a laugh.

They paused at the top of the stairs, and Paige smiled up at Colin. In his white T-shirt and brown suede jacket, he was looking fairly billboard worthy, but it wasn't just his gorgeousness that she found attractive. Paige had spent all afternoon daydreaming about this guy and over the course of the evening, the real him had managed to blow the daydream him right out of the water. Not only had he called the very night he had gotten her number, but he had picked the perfect place for their first date—a secluded restaurant with vines of bright flowers lining the walls and candlelight flickering from every corner. Plus, unlike most guys, who spent ninety percent of the night talking about themselves, Colin had asked Paige all kinds of questions about *her* life. He seemed genuinely interested in getting to know her, not just getting her to kiss him.

Of course, now she wanted to kiss him. She wanted to kiss him really, *really* badly.

"So . . . ," Paige said, her smile widening.

"So . . . ," Colin replied. Was it just her, or was he staring at her lips?

Paige took a step closer to him. The air around them seemed to sizzle. A light breeze tossed the hair hanging down her back and sent a pleasant shiver through her body. Paige enjoyed the heightened sensations. Just being around Colin made everything more vivid.

"I had an incredible time," she said.

"So did I," Colin replied, his voice a near-whisper. "It was . . . magical."

Paige froze. The kiss-me-now daze faded away faster than she could say "danger." Magical? Why would he choose to use that word above any others?

If I just got scammed by a demon or a warlock I am going to go kung fu all over him, Paige thought, clenching her jaw.

"What?" Colin asked. "Is everything okay?"

There was a hint of concern in his brown eyes. Or was there? Paige searched his face, trying to read behind his eyes, inside his heart. He had been such a perfect gentleman all night long—charming, funny, polite. He got all her jokes and even finished a couple of her sentences. He opened doors, offered to share his food, made sure she wasn't too warm or too cold in the car. She couldn't think of a single negative about him. The evening had been perfect.

Of course, if he turned out to be a force of evil, it would definitely put a damper on things.

If only she could recite a revelation spell right there and bring out the demon's real face. On the other hand, if she recited the spell and he turned out to be just a plain old human, she would have some serious explaining to do. Not a lot of women make up supernatural poetry at the end of a date.

Nope. She needed some backup.

"Could you just . . . wait here for a sec?" Paige asked, grasping the heavy doorknob. "I want to see if my sisters are home. I think they may want to meet you."

Colin's face brightened. "Great! I'd love to meet them."

"I'll be right back," Paige said. Then she slipped through the front door and leaned back against it, taking a deep breath. "Yeah. I'll bet you want to meet them. Little demon bastard."

Paige sighed and went in search of her sisters.

"Come on, Wyatt," Phoebe cajoled. "Roll the ball to Aunt Phoebe! Roll the ball to Aunt Phoebe, Wyatt."

Piper Halliwell smirked as her son grasped his red plastic ball and stared at Phoebe like she was asking him to give up bottles for life. Phoebe and Wyatt were sitting across from each other on the floor of the sunroom, toys strewn all around them. They had been playing for over an hour while Piper straightened up the house and went over the books from her nightclub, P3. Sometimes it was really nice having two live-in babysitters. Piper dropped Wyatt's teddy bear into his playpen and tossed her long dark hair over her shoulder.

"Come on, Wyatt," she said, crouching down. "Roley Poley, remember?"

Wyatt shook his head and hugged the ball even harder.

"I don't think he wants to play anymore," Piper said.

Phoebe's brow creased. "He's looking at me like he thinks I'm the enemy," she said.

"Well, what do you expect when you're trying to take his ball away?" Piper joked.

"I'm not trying to take your ball away, sweetie," Phoebe said, leaning forward and shaking her head as she smiled. "No, I'm not. I just want to play."

Wyatt glanced over at his playpen. Suddenly his teddy bear disappeared in a swirl of white light and reappeared in Phoebe's arms. Phoebe's mouth dropped open and she looked at Piper, who cracked up laughing.

"I guess he thinks you should play with that instead," Piper said.

"Tricky little fella," Phoebe said, narrowing her eyes.

Wyatt cracked a smile and brought the ball up to his mouth. Phoebe smiled and hugged the teddy bear.

"Thanks, Wyatt," she said, reaching out to run her fingers over his blond hair. "I know this is your favorite."

Piper planted a kiss on top of her magical son's head and leaned back. She checked her watch, then glanced toward the front windows. "I wonder how Paige's date is going."

At that moment the front door slammed. "Looks like we're about to find out," Phoebe said.

Piper lifted Wyatt, and she and Phoebe stood up just as Paige stalked into the room. She was wearing her favorite little black dress and her hair was pulled back from her flushed face. There was an air of charged panic about her that sent Piper's radar off.

"Hey," she said. "Everything go okay?"

"Not exactly," Paige said, dropping her silver purse on the couch and flopping down next to it. "I think he may be a warlock."

"Oh, no," Phoebe said. "Honey, I'm sorry."

"Wouldn't be the first time for this family," Piper said. "Or the second . . . or the tenth. . . ."

"What are you going to do?" Phoebe asked, sitting next to Paige.

"Actually, I was hoping you guys could help me test him," Paige said, biting her bottom lip. "Just to make sure."

"Yeah. We could do that. We could invite him over for brunch tomorrow, maybe try something then," Piper said, shifting Wyatt to her other hip.

"Or we could do it right now," Paige suggested. "He's kind of standing on the front step."

Piper's heart caught at the idea of a potential demon lingering outside the house. It was a feeling she would never get used to. "He's still here?"

"Well, I didn't want to send him home," Paige told them, lifting a hand. "If he is mortal, he's like, the most perfect guy on the planet."

Piper glanced at Phoebe, bouncing Wyatt up and down. "All right. What can we do that's not too obvious?"

"The enchantment spell?" Phoebe asked with a shrug. "Remember, it reveals the evil within? If there is any, of course. It's better than freezing him and pricking him with a pin to see if he bleeds."

"Yeah. The invisible mosquito excuse is getting kind of old," Piper agreed.

Years before, the sisters had found out that warlocks didn't bleed, so they had come up with a test for their potential boyfriends. Piper would freeze the guy, then they would prick him with a pin, and then Piper would unfreeze him. If blood appeared, that meant the guy was human. Of course, he was also left wondering why he had what looked like a pinprick on his arm when nothing had touched him.

"Got your sunglasses on you?" Phoebe asked Paige.

Paige reached into her purse and pulled out her gold-tinted shades, handing them over.

"Okay, we'll enchant the glasses. You go get him off the front step before the neighbors start thinking we've got a stalker," Piper said.

"Thanks, you guys," Paige said.

She scurried off, and Piper put Wyatt down in the playpen. As always, Wyatt stood up and gripped the sides of the pen, watching his mom and aunt with interest. Piper and Phoebe placed the sunglasses on the table and touched the frames with their fingertips.

"Sounds like she really likes this guy," Phoebe said.

"Yeah. Let's just hope we don't have to vanquish him," Piper replied.

Together, they recited the spell.

> *Magic forces far and wide,*
> *enchant these so those can't hide.*
> *Allow this witch to use therein,*
> *So she can reveal the evil within.*

The door closed again and Piper slipped the sunglasses on. She felt slightly nuts wearing sunglasses inside when it was well past sundown, but it didn't really matter. All that mattered was helping Paige find out the truth about her new crush. Piper and Phoebe stood up straight as Paige walked through the door, followed by her date.

"Oh my God," Piper said automatically, her heart responding with a violent thump.

Paige took an instinctive step away from Colin, and Phoebe grasped Piper's hand.

"What is it? Demon? Warlock? Is it hideous?" Phoebe whispered, turning her back to Colin.

Piper turned around also and removed the glasses, fanning her face with her free hand. "Oh, no. He's human. It's just . . . did she tell us he was that beautiful?" she asked.

Phoebe rolled her eyes and turned Piper around again, laughing in obvious embarrassment. "Hi!" she said, offering her hand to Paige's date. "You must be Colin. I'm Phoebe."

Luckily, Colin seemed unfazed by any weirdness. "Nice to meet you," he said, shaking her hand. "And you're Piper, then?"

Piper grinned and nodded. She couldn't stop grinning, in fact. This was very unlike her. She couldn't remember the last time a hot guy had such an effect on her insides. Not that she would ever do anything about it. After all, she was a happily married wife and mother. But that didn't mean she couldn't appreciate perfection when she saw it. Paige sure knew how to pick 'em.

"Everything *okay*, you guys?" Paige asked pointedly.

"Yes! Everything is just fine!" Piper replied. "Totally normal. Nothing to worry about."

Paige's face registered relief, but then she shot Piper a look that said, *If everything's normal, then stop acting like a freak!*

"And who's this little guy?" Colin asked, crouching next to the playpen.

Another test passed. Wyatt had his very own protective force field that always went up when demons and warlocks were around. When Colin bent over him, Wyatt merely looked up at him curiously.

"That's Piper's son, Wyatt," Phoebe replied, joining him.

Oh my God! Piper mouthed to Paige the second his back was turned. She dropped her jaw for dramatic effect. *He's incredible!*

I know! Paige mouthed back. *Not a demon?*

Piper handed Paige the sunglasses so she could see for herself. Paige slipped the glasses on, glanced at Colin's profile, then smiled and tossed the shades onto the couch. Glancing up at the ceiling, she mouthed a quick *thank you*. Piper knew the feeling. She couldn't count how many times in the past either she or her sisters had gone through the same uncertainty. As the Charmed Ones, they couldn't trust any guy who happened to drop into their lives.

But at least this one was human. And Paige was clearly very into him. Now all Piper could do was hope that he wouldn't somehow manage to break her sister's heart.

Chapter Two

Paige walked down the concrete aisle steps at SBC Stadium, following behind Colin and the usher who was leading them to their seats. On the field the crack of the bat was followed by a huge roar from the crowd, as everyone around her jumped to their feet. For a split second Paige was worried she would lose Colin in the mayhem, but then she realized it would be impossible. How did you lose someone who was carrying a Giants pennant, a huge blow-up baseball bat, *and* an orange foam finger?

"Right here," the usher said, pausing next to a pair of box seats in the third row.

"You're kidding. Here?" Paige asked.

Normally when she came to baseball games she was so high in the nosebleeds that the bases looked like mini marshmallows. From here she could see the dirt on the first baseman's backside.

Colin sat down in his seat and grinned happily up at her.

"Wow. These are some seats," Paige said as the usher hustled back up to the entryway. She sat down next to Colin and took the box of popcorn he held out to her. "How did you get these? Are you a millionaire or something?"

Out on the field the umpire shouted, "Strike!" Paige raised her eyebrows. She had never been close enough to the field to hear the umpire before.

"Paige, I have a confession to make," Colin said.

Oh, no, here it comes. He's married. These seats belong to his wife's family or something, Paige thought. "Okay. What is it?" she asked, holding her breath.

"These aren't my seats," Colin said. "I got them from an old friend."

"Oh, well, that's no big deal," Paige said, inwardly sighing with relief. "Season tickets to the Giants are not a deal breaker for me."

"No. That's not the confession," Colin said, flushing. "The confession is, I've never been to a baseball game before."

Paige took in Colin's outfit—brand-new Giants windbreaker, Giants hat, and all the souvenirs—and found this confession easy to believe.

"Wow. You mean your parents never took you to a single game?" she asked.

"My parents are very busy people," Colin told her as a ball was popped up foul. "They don't really have time for . . . fun."

Paige tossed a piece of popcorn into her mouth. This was the first time Colin had mentioned his family and she was intrigued. A little sharing of personal info meant he was feeling closer to her.

"What do your parents do that keeps them so busy?" Paige asked.

The second the question was out of her mouth, she realized that Colin had never even told her what *he* did for a living. She didn't mind avoiding the topic, since she didn't have much to share on her own end, but now that they were on the second date, curiosity was starting to nibble at her.

"They . . . well . . . they run a small . . . family business," Colin said, taking a sip of his soda. "In fact, sooner or later they expect me to take it over."

"Why do I sense that you're not so happy about that prospect?" Paige asked, narrowing her eyes slightly.

"Because you're very intuitive," Colin said, flashing that heart-stopping grin. "No, it's not that I don't want to. It's just that . . . well . . . there are a lot of sacrifices involved when it comes to carrying on a family legacy. Do you know what I mean?"

His brown eyes locked on hers, and Paige felt a funny swirl of intrigue and familiarity in her chest.

"Oh yeah," she said, thinking of her Charmed destiny. "I know exactly what you mean."

Suddenly there was another loud *crack* from the field and everyone looked up. Paige registered the fact that a foul ball was flying straight at her face, but somehow restrained herself from orbing it away.

This is going to hurt, she thought, trying to duck out of the line of fire, even though her brain recognized that there was no time.

Then, at the last millisecond, Colin leaned over her and plucked the ball right out of the air.

"Ugh!" he shouted in pain, tossing the ball to his other hand and shaking out his fingers.

"Colin! Are you okay?" Paige asked, pulling his wrist toward her. His palm and fingers were bright red from the impact.

"I'm fine," Colin said, grimacing as the fans around him slapped his back in congratulations.

"Nice catch, man," a chubby guy behind them said, scratching his head in awe.

"That ball almost rearranged your girlfriend's face!" someone else shouted.

"Yeah," Paige said, her heart still racing. "You pretty much just saved me there."

Colin smiled and shrugged, pocketing the ball. "Wouldn't be much of a date if we ended up in the emergency room."

"My hero," she said jokingly, slipping her arm around his.

"Yeah. Let's see if you get home in one piece

first before you start calling me that," Colin joked back. "Apparently, when you pay for the good seats, you also pay for the thrill of not knowing whether you'll get beaned."

"We're fine," Paige said, settling in. "There's nothing to worry about."

As she watched the batter step back into the box, Paige realized that this was the first time in forever that she could sit back on a date and actually feel like that was true. There was nothing for her to worry about. With Colin she felt safe, relaxed, comfortable, and happy. He had gotten her sisters' seal of approval the other night, and he had yet to do or say one thing to make her doubt him. Paige smiled at his profile as he watched the game, riveted. Her heart fluttered with anticipation and excitement.

Had she really done it? Had she actually found her Prince Charming?

Phoebe sat at the table in the sunroom, typing away at her laptop computer. Piper was at P3 and Wyatt was playing on the floor near Phoebe, busily building towers out of blocks and then gleefully knocking them down. In the background the news was showing on the TV, turned down to a moderate volume. Phoebe's editor at the *Bay Mirror*, Elise, was attending a charity event that evening and had a shot at getting on the evening broadcast. If so, Phoebe didn't want to miss it. Elise hated it when she got her face on TV and no one at the office noticed.

On the table around Phoebe's computer lay stacks of letters and printed-out e-mails from people in various states of dismay about love, life, family, or work. She had divided them into three categories: "Needy, but not needy enough," "Needy enough to need my help," and "So needy that not even a team of shrinks could do anything." She was currently working on answering the dilemma explained in the top letter on the "Needy enough to need my help" pile. Written in looping script on light blue stationery, it was the story of a girl who had met the man of her dreams, only to have her ex-boyfriend reappear in the picture, promising to make everything right. "Torn in Oakland" wanted to know if she should stick with her new man or give the ex a second chance.

If your ex-boyfriend never kept his promises to you in the past, there's no reason to believe that he will now. He's obviously just trying to win you back because he's jealous, Phoebe typed, her fingers pounding vehemently against the keys. *Your new man sounds like a guy who loves you, supports you, and takes care of you. Why would you even think about giving that up?*

On the floor next to her, Wyatt let out a little squeal as he knocked over his latest tower. The noise startled Phoebe out of her advice-giving zone and she leaned back, letting out a deep breath. She took a sip of her tea and read over what she'd just written.

"Too harsh?" she asked, looking down at Wyatt.

He responded by picking up a blue block and laughing.

"Yeah. Too harsh," Phoebe said, deleting the last line.

"For the third day in a row, torrential downpours plagued central Switzerland, causing flooding and forcing people from their homes," the newscaster announced. *"The storms have meteorologists stumped."*

The television cut to an interview with an elderly man explaining why, exactly, the weather in Switzerland was so bizarre. Phoebe checked her watch. The newscast would be over in five minutes. Apparently Elise wasn't getting the screen time she craved.

"Okay, how do I tell 'Torn in Oakland' to wake up and smell the jealousy without sounding like I'm knocking her over the head?" Phoebe asked.

Wyatt tossed the blue block at her, and Phoebe caught it out of the air before it could smack her in the temple. "I said I *didn't* want to knock her over the head," she told him, sliding out of her chair and handing him the block. "But you've got a good arm there, kid. If the whole most-powerful-being-in-the-universe thing doesn't work out, you might have a future in the NFL."

A swirl of orbs appeared just behind Wyatt and suddenly Leo was standing there, smiling down at his son.

"There's my boy," he said, leaning down to pick up Wyatt. "Hey, Phoebe. How's the babysitting going?"

"Great. We were just talking about his prospects as a starting QB," Phoebe said, standing. "The kid's throwing bombs."

Leo's handsome face brightened. "Yeah? You gonna play for the Forty-niners, Wyatt? They could use all the help they can get," he said, bringing his nose to his son's. Wyatt laughed and touched his tiny hands to Leo's face.

"Where's Paige?" Leo asked, glancing around.

"Oh, out with Colin," she said, waving a hand in the air.

"Again?" Leo asked, his brow rising.

"Third date in four days," Phoebe told him with a nod. "Yesterday he took her to a Giants game, and then they had a picnic dinner in the mountains. Could be something."

"Sounds like it," Leo said.

Phoebe smiled as Leo brought Wyatt over to the playpen and placed him down. Just thinking of Paige starting up a healthy, happy relationship made Phoebe all bubbly inside. Her little sister deserved some romance, and Colin seemed like just the guy to give it to her.

"So, what's up?" Phoebe asked Leo. "To what do I owe the honor of this orb-in?"

As Leo turned around again, he adopted that all-business expression. The one that always spelled supernatural trouble.

"Uh-oh," Phoebe said, pushing her hands into the back pockets of her jeans. "What's going on?"

"It's the Elders. They've sensed a shift in the balance of power," Leo said. "A big shift."

"The balance of power?" Phoebe asked. "You mean, like, the balance of power between good and evil?"

"Yeah. That one," Leo said.

"That's a big one," Phoebe replied.

"Tell me about it. They say there's a huge center of dark mystical forces gathering over in Europe," Leo said. "Apparently, no one up there has ever felt anything like this before. They don't know what to make of it."

"It's never good when it's something the Elders have never felt before," Phoebe said. She glanced over Leo's shoulder at the reporter on the TV, who was being knocked around by gale-force winds and driving rain.

"Officials in Switzerland are considering calling a state of emergency, and both the UN and the American Red Cross have already dispatched aid to the storm-ravaged area. . . ."

"Leo, these dark mystical forces . . . they wouldn't be gathering in, oh . . . say . . . Switzerland, would they?" Phoebe asked, her intuition piqued.

"Yeah, actually. Why?" Leo asked.

Phoebe pointed at the TV as the image shifted to a line of houses that were half underwater. Whole families sat on rooftops waiting for rescue. Apparently there *was* an explanation for the unexplainable storms. . . .

This is too good to be true, Paige's more logical half tried to tell her. *Colin has to be a mirage. Either that, or this is some long, drawn-out, blissful dream. There's no way this guy is real.*

"More champagne?" Colin asked, lifting the bottle of Cristal out of the ice bucket.

Paige nodded and smiled, watching the candlelight dance in his eyes while he poured. Under the table, she pinched her own leg, then tried not to wince. She was definitely awake.

"This place is beautiful," she said, taking a sip of her champagne.

The restaurant was small and cozy, the gleaming oak walls hung with tapestries in thick red and maize. Deep red tablecloths covered the tables, and the silverware wasn't silver at all, but gleaming gold. Even the champagne flutes had gold stems, and the china was rimmed in gold. Paige felt as if she were dining in a Victorian novel as each course was served by an older gentleman in a three-piece tuxedo. Even the clientele looked more distinguished, more sophisticated than the usual San Francisco crowds.

"Only more so because you're here," Colin said, replacing the bottle.

Paige smirked even as her face flushed with pleasure. "Nice line," she said.

"Why do you always think everything I say is a line?" Colin asked.

"Because everything you say is too good to be true," Paige replied.

"You know that's not the case," Colin replied. "You light up every room you walk into."

Paige smirked again.

"I know, I know," Colin said, raising his hands in surrender. "Nice line."

Paige laughed and lifted her glass to clink with Colin's. She was trying to play it cool, but inside she was a mess of butterflies. Her mind was conjuring up images it had never conjured before. Paige in a gorgeous white wedding gown. Paige and Colin walking down the aisle, laughing as rose petals showered around them. Paige and Colin moving boxes into a house in the hills above town, then bringing home their firstborn child.

Of course, the question would be what to tell the daddy when the kid started orbing his bottles into his crib. Colin didn't know Paige was a witch, but even if it wasn't too early for fantasies, it was far too early for that revelation.

This is just your fourth date, Paige reminded herself. There was plenty of time to figure out how to hurdle her magical little obstacle. For now, she was enjoying her daydreams.

I can really see myself with this guy, she thought as Colin took a bite of his filet mignon. *How insane is that?*

"Another bottle, monsieur?" the waiter asked, appearing soundlessly at their side.

Colin smiled. "Yes, I think we'll be needing more."

"I don't know about that," Paige said. "I think I'm already feeling this bottle."

Colin swallowed hard and cleared his throat. He looked a little pale all of a sudden, and Paige's heart skipped a worried beat.

"Are you all right?" she asked, leaning forward.

"I'm fine," Colin said, looking into her eyes. "Perfect, actually."

"Good, because you scared me there for a second," Paige said. "Serious face on a date is never a good sign."

"Paige, there's something I need to do," Colin said.

Then, in one perfectly fluid motion, he stood up, reached into his pocket, dropped to one knee next to her, and pulled out a small velvet box. Paige's heart completely stopped as everyone in the room turned to gape at them. This couldn't be happening. It just couldn't be.

"Okay, now you're *really* scaring me," Paige said.

Colin opened the box and there, gleaming up at her, was the single most gorgeous diamond ring Paige had ever laid eyes on. She pinched herself under the table again, hard, and actually winced at the pain. Maybe this really was happening.

"Paige Matthews, I know this is kind of sudden, but the past few days have been the most amazing days of my life," Colin said.

"Colin—"

He ignored her and kept right on going. "And I promise that I will spend the rest of my life making *your* days just as amazing," he said. "Paige, will you marry me?"

"Okay, now I know that was a line," Paige said, trying to break the extreme confusion and tension with a joke.

"Wrong again," Colin said, his eyes hopeful. "I'm dead serious here."

"Colin, we barely know each other," Paige said. "This is just insane."

But the movie of their wedding was playing itself in the back of her mind. The pictures of the two of them together, happy, making a life. People had done crazier things than this, hadn't they?

"I know we just met, Paige, but I feel like we were meant to be together," Colin told her. "And I know you feel it too. I just don't want to let a chance like this slip by."

Paige's whole body was shaking. Her mouth

was dry. *I could say yes*, she thought wildly. *I could actually say yes to him.*

"So?" Colin asked, his eyes full of hope. "What do you say? Paige Matthews, will you be my wife?"

Chapter Three

Paige looked into Colin's eyes, her pulse racing. Everyone in the restaurant was watching them, holding their breath. An older woman to her left smiled at Paige, her eyes watery with happy tears. Time ceased to move. Paige knew she had to say something, but her mind seemed unable to focus on anything. She just couldn't believe this was happening. She couldn't believe she was being proposed to, and she had no idea what to say. When she opened her mouth to speak, she decided she would just go with whatever came out.

"Colin, I just think this is a little too fast," Paige replied.

Even though his eyes registered disappointment and Paige's heart went out to him, she was happy to see that her brain was still functioning on a logical level. Colin was a great guy, but as much as he had her believing in love at first sight, she knew it wasn't the kind of love they could build a life on. It was a romantic thing, an infatuation, a major, major crush. She had to know someone longer than four days before agreeing to spend the rest of her life with him. Of course, Colin didn't seem to appreciate or even hear her logic. He was still down on one knee, extending the ring.

"Can't we just date for a little while?" Paige asked. "You know, see where it all—"

"Colin! What are you doing?"

Paige's head snapped up. Colin automatically covered his eyes with his free hand—the one not holding an engagement ring—as if somehow he had expected this to happen. Stalking across the restaurant was a tall, gorgeous blond woman who, though raggedy around the edges, very casually dressed, and clearly in desperate need of some sleep, was as perfect as a supermodel. Even in the stunned quiet of the restaurant, it took Paige a moment to fully realize that this runway-worthy goddess was talking about *her* date. *Her* potential fiancé. When the blonde finally arrived at the table, Paige slumped back in her chair.

"I knew this was too good to be true," Paige said. "Who are you?"

"I'm his fiancée."

"What?" Paige blurted.

I can't believe this. I can't believe that even Colin is one of those *guys,* Paige thought, clenching her teeth. *Who the hell goes out and proposes to someone when he already has a fiancée?*

"How could you come here without even *telling* me?" the girl ranted, dropping to her knees next to Colin, who was still in proposal pose. "Do you have any idea how worried I've been?"

Even in the mass confusion, and struggling with her growing ire, Paige realized that these were odd things to say to your fiancé when he was in the process of proposing to someone else. Where was the "You lying, cheating, jerk!" followed by a glass of wine in the face? Was this girl really saying that she had been *worried* about this pig? Didn't she realize what was going on here?

"Corinne, I'm sorry. But you know I had no choice," Colin said, getting to his feet.

"The least you could have done was given me the courtesy of talking to me about it," the girl, Corinne, replied as he pulled her up as well. "You know, giving me a heads-up that you were asking her to marry you today! We're supposed to talk about everything. . . ."

Feeling invisible and quite used, Paige sat up straight and waved her hand. "Hello? Anyone feel like telling me what the heck is going on?"

Colin and Corinne both looked down at her as if they had forgotten she was there. This was rich.

"Paige," she said slowly, laying a hand on her chest. "I'm Paige, remember? The girl you were just offering that ring to?"

Suddenly the maître d' appeared at Colin's side, his hands clasped together and his brow dotted with sweat. He gave a slight bow, his expression desperate.

"Excuse me, sir. I'm sorry, but the other customers . . ."

Colin blinked and looked around the room. Everyone in the place was either gaping at him in disapproval or pointedly staring at their meals trying to avoid eye contact and pretend nothing unusual was going on. Paige raised her eyebrows. She couldn't blame any of them. This whole evening was turning into a major train wreck.

Why do I even bother dating? she thought. *Every time I go out with someone it just gets worse and worse.*

"Of course," Colin said, snapping the jewelry box closed on the engagement ring and pocketing it. "Ladies, shall we take this outside?"

"I have a better idea," Paige said, standing and grabbing her purse. "How about you two stay and finish dinner? I'm out of here."

She swept by Colin and his supposed fiancée, heading for the door as fast as her high heels would allow. She couldn't believe she had thought Colin was actually different, and he had turned out to be worse than all of the guys she had ever dated in her entire life put together. Already engaged? What was *wrong* with him?

That's it. I'm never dating again, Paige said to

herself. *I'm going to be an old spinster and I'm going to be proud of my singlehood . . . and my many cats.*

It wasn't until she'd pushed open the heavy wooden door and stepped out into the cool night air that she remembered she had no way of getting home. Colin had driven her here in his Jaguar. Or maybe it was Corinne's Jaguar. Suddenly everything about him seemed false.

They were all lines, Paige realized suddenly, feeling beyond ashamed that just moments ago she had thought that their wordplay was cute.

Paige groaned and was about to orb home when the door behind her swung open again. Colin and his woman were coming right at her, but she ignored them and started to walk away. She was either going to find a cab or find a deserted spot to orb from, whichever came first.

"Paige," Colin said, grabbing her shoulder as he caught up to her. "Would you please let me explain?"

Paige tore her arm away and glared at him. "Are you kidding me? What possible explanation could you have for asking me to marry you when you already have a fiancée?" She turned and looked at Corinne, who was standing next to him, looking upset but not livid. "And you! Why are you not beating him over the head with your bag right now?"

Colin and Corinne shared a look that made Paige feel like a totally clueless outsider. Then Corinne shrugged.

"You tell her," she said. "This was your brilliant plan." Then she turned away slightly while Colin blew out a resigned sigh.

"What? What brilliant plan?" Paige asked, anger throbbing in her veins. "What the hell is going on here?"

"Okay, look. Corinne *is* my fiancée, but we can't get married," Colin said.

"Why not?" Paige asked.

"Because I have to marry another magical being in order to guarantee the safety of my kingdom and the citizens who live within its walls," Colin said.

Paige blinked. "Come again?"

"I have to marry another magical—"

"No! I heard you . . . I heard you," Paige said, shaking her head. She shifted her weight from one foot to the other, trying to process this new information. "So, wait a minute. You're a magical being? What are you?"

"He's a witch," Corinne put in. "A good witch."

Paige stared at her. "And you are . . . ?"

"Not," Corinne said. "Which is kind of the problem."

Another couple stepped out of the restaurant, and Colin took both women by their arms and led them around the corner to a more secluded spot. This time Paige didn't shy away from his touch. She was too busy wondering if he was a total psycho and if she should just orb away right now before his ax murderer side came out. A good witch she could believe. She had met plenty of those in her lifetime. But what was all this about a kingdom?

Paige stepped behind a flowering tree at the corner of the restaurant and glanced around. Aside from the valets half a block away near the entrance to the parking lot, there was no one in sight.

"Okay, you better start talking, fast," Paige said.

"What do you want us to say?" Corinne asked.

"Something that will convince me not to vanquish your butts or call the paddy wagon," Paige said. "What kingdom are we talking about here?"

"We come from a magical realm called Tarsina," Colin said. "It exists on an alternate plane and it's invisible to the mortal eye. My parents are the king and queen, which makes me—"

"The prince," Paige said, hardly able to believe what she was hearing. "That's what you meant when you were talking about taking over the family business?"

"Yeah," Colin said, gritting his teeth slightly as if to apologize.

"I thought you owned a bakery or a car wash or something."

Corinne snorted a laugh, and Paige, much to

her surprise, found that she was able to smile. "Go on," she said.

"Well, if I don't marry another magical being by my twenty-fifth birthday, the curse my great-great-grandmother put on the kingdom will come to fruition and all the mortals who have come to live in Tarsina over the years will die," Colin said.

Paige would have sat down if there was anywhere to do it. She felt like she was listening to a fairy tale, except the characters were standing right in front of her. A few years ago she would have told these people they were crazy, but now she knew that pretty much anything was possible. Paige had actually *lived* a couple of fairy tales already. The existence of another wasn't too much to swallow.

"So you're a mortal," Paige said, looking at Corinne.

"Yep. Just a plain old regular person," Corinne replied, raising her hands.

"So you weren't thinking about this curse when you proposed to her, then, were ya?" Paige said sarcastically.

Colin looked at Corinne and reached out for her hand, which she gave without hesitation. As Paige watched them gazing into each other's eyes and saw the deep sadness between them, her heart squeezed in her chest. Ten minutes ago she had been thinking about having a perfect future with this guy. Now it was abundantly clear that he was meant for someone else.

"I wasn't thinking about anything," Colin said. "Except how much I love her."

I'm going to be sick, Paige thought. *This guy totally used me.*

"That would be sweet if I didn't want to wring your neck right about now," Paige said. A dozen emotions were warring for attention inside of her—everything from sympathy for the star-crossed lovers, to disappointment for herself, to total blinding anger. It was exhausting.

"I'm really sorry, Paige," Colin said, swallowing hard. "But we really do need your help."

"You know what? This is a little too much for me to handle," Paige told them. "Hold on, you two. We're going on a little trip."

She placed one hand on each of their shoulders and orbed them out of there as quickly as possible. This was a dilemma that definitely required a little sisterly advice.

"So they don't know what it is and they don't know how to deal with it, but they would just like us to be aware of the problem," Piper said. She paced across the living room, stopped, and crossed her arms over her chest, her brow creasing as she looked at her husband. "Do you think they could vague that up for us a little?"

Leo raised his shoulders. "What do you want me to say? I'm just telling you what I know."

"That dark magic is gathering over Switzerland," Phoebe said, leaning her head on the back of the couch. "Isn't Switzerland supposed to be neutral?"

Piper smirked. "Nah. Those Swiss love a little dark magic when they can get their hands on it."

Just as she was saying this, Paige orbed right into the room with Colin and a tall female stranger. It was clear from the looks on their faces that they had just heard exactly what Piper had said, but it didn't matter all that much. If Paige was orbing people around the city, the Charmed Ones' secret had already been blown.

"Paige? What're you doing orbing your new boyfriend in here?" Piper asked through her teeth, walking over to her little sister.

"Phoebe, Piper, Leo, I'd like you to meet Colin, the crown prince of Tarsina," Paige said, lifting her hands toward her date. "And this is Corinne." She looked from Phoebe to Piper and pursed her lips. "His *fiancée*."

Piper's jaw dropped, and Paige slumped onto the couch as if the life had been sucked right out of her.

"Hi," Corinne said awkwardly, waving a hand and then quickly shoving it back into the pocket of her cargo pants.

"Hello. Nice to meet you," Piper said slowly. "Now do either of you want to explain?"

"Which part?" Colin asked, looking like the proverbial deer in the headlights.

"All of it," Phoebe suggested.

"Yeah. I thought Tarsina was a myth," Leo said, clearly intrigued.

"You knew about this place?" Paige demanded.

"Well . . . yeah," Leo said. "But no one I know has ever been there. I just figured it was one of those fairy-tale things, like—"

"Cinderella?" Phoebe said, raising her eyebrows. She had, in fact, *been* Cinderella once.

"Or the Evil Enchantress?" Paige added. The villain from one of her favorite stories had turned out to be Paige herself—in a past life.

"Or leprechauns, perhaps?" Piper put in, tilting her head. At this point the Charmed Ones knew more leprechauns than they cared to count.

"All right, all right. I get it," Leo said, raising his arms in surrender. "Tarsina is real." He sat on the arm of the couch and looked up at Colin, as eager as a kid on Santa's lap. "So what's it like?" he asked, his eyes bright with anticipation.

"It's beautiful," Colin said. "Just as you would expect it to be. But right now it's under serious threat. That dark magic you were speaking of when we came in? I know what that's all about."

"We know a little too well," Corinne said, sitting down on the edge of the antique chair that stood across from the couch.

"You see, Tarsina existed for centuries untouched and unadulterated by nonmagical beings. It's invisible to the eyes of mortals . . . well . . . except those who are invited in by one of the kingdom's residents," Colin explained, warming to his subject. "Then, early in the twentieth century, Tarsina's people started to venture out. We started to explore. And little by little, the citizens brought back evidence of the outside world. Cars and radios popped up all over the kingdom. And later we had TVs, cameras, even the Internet."

"Don't tell me. Some people didn't like the fact that the modern world was invading your space," Phoebe put in. "I just don't get the anti-techie vibe," she added, shaking her head.

"It wasn't the innovations. It was the people," Corinne explained, clasping her hands between her knees. "Some of the Tarsinians brought back mortal husbands and wives. That was what caused the problem."

Piper and Leo exchanged a look. She and her Whitelighter husband knew all too well about the closed-mindedness of some people when it came to certain love matches.

"My great-great-grandmother, who was then the queen, was appalled," Colin said with a nod. "She didn't think nonmagic blood should mix with ours. She didn't want nonmagical people living within our walls, but she couldn't expel them without risking the wrath of the population. She *could* ensure, however, that her own line remained pure."

"The curse," Paige said slowly.

Piper's heart skipped a beat. "The curse?" she repeated, looking at her sister. "What curse? Have you gotten yourself involved in some kind of curse?"

"No, Piper. I'm fine," Paige said. "At least so far," she added under her breath.

Piper narrowed her eyes at Paige before returning her attention to Colin and Corinne. She did not like the direction in which this was going, but there was no turning back now.

"Before she died in 1916, the old hag put a curse on the kingdom," Corinne explained, standing again. "Each heir to the throne must marry another pure magical being by his or her twenty-fifth birthday or her wrath will rain down on the kingdom." She stepped up to Colin, and he put his arm around her. "They say only those of pure magical blood will be spared."

"That means thousands of people will die," Colin said. "Including Corinne and her father."

A heavy silence fell over the living room. Piper's heart felt like it was turning to stone within her. She had heard this story too many times before—two people in love, unable to be together because of someone else's stupid beliefs. And this time a whole population would suffer for it. It was beyond unfair. It was ridiculous.

"When's your twenty-fifth birthday?" Phoebe asked finally.

Colin took a deep breath and looked at Paige. "Wednesday."

Paige was out of her seat like a shot. "You expected to woo me and marry me by Wednesday?" she blurted. "Do I really look that desperate to you?"

Piper put a comforting hand on her sister's arm. Freaking out did not seem like the best plan at the moment, but she understood what her sister was feeling. That afternoon she had been gushing about how amazing Colin was. This whole story must have come as not only a shock, but a serious disappointment.

"I'm so sorry, Paige," Colin said, reaching for her hands. "I had heard of the all-powerful, benevolent Charmed Ones and I guess I thought that if I could get one of you to care for me . . . and then I told you my story . . . you would never turn me down."

Corinne stared at Paige's hands enveloped in Colin's until she saw that Piper was watching her, and she turned away. Clearly Corinne was devastated to see the love of her life touching another woman in such an intimate way. Piper's heart went out to her—to all of them. This was an impossible situation.

"All-powerful and benevolent, maybe," Paige said, withdrawing her hands. "But I don't know if I can marry someone who's in love with someone else, Colin," she added, looking at the ground.

"Why didn't you just tell us the truth from the beginning?" Phoebe asked.

"I don't know," Colin said, lifting one shoulder. He looked so exhausted, so sorry. "I was desperate. I don't think I fully knew what I was doing. All I knew was that I was running out of time."

"So why wait so long?" Leo asked. "You've known about this curse your whole life. Why wait until now to find a magical bride?"

"That was my fault," Corinne said, slipping her hand into Colin's. "We fell in love, and you know what that's like. You think you can overcome anything. So we spent months trying to figure out a way around the curse. Something that would allow us to marry. We asked everyone—everyone who would understand, that is."

"It was only a week ago that we finally resigned ourselves to the fact that there were no loopholes," Colin said. "We can be in love, but we can't get married."

"And then he disappeared," Corinne added. "I had a friend scry for him and she found him here. I don't have any magical powers, so I had to take three different flights just to follow him. I'm okay with the plan—but I didn't expect to see him proposing to you. Not without telling me first."

"I'm so sorry," Colin said to Corinne, squeezing her hand. "I know you were worried. I just didn't know what else to do."

Corinne smiled with tears in her eyes and kissed Colin on the cheek. Piper could tell all was forgiven, but nothing forgotten. She knew firsthand what it was like to be clinging to a person who could be taken away at any moment. It wasn't a pleasant way to live.

"And I apologize to you, too, Paige," Colin said. "To all of you. I never wanted to lie to anyone, I swear it. It's just . . . my people are counting on me."

"He's right," Corinne said, putting on a brave face. "He has to marry someone else to save our people. So many of our friends, so many innocent families . . . their lives are depending on him. As much as I hate it, I've accepted that this is the only way."

Piper looked at Paige, whose skin was about as white as a wedding dress. This wasn't a fair thing to ask of her, or of anyone.

"Paige?" Piper said.

"At least come and see Tarsina before you turn me down," Colin implored. "You'll see it's a real place, an amazing place. You'll see how kind and good the people are. I know you'll want to help."

Paige looked around at her family, and Leo tilted his head and raised his eyebrows, suggesting a private Halliwell conference.

"Excuse us," Piper said as Phoebe pushed herself off the couch. They trailed Leo into the front hallway and huddled up into a circle.

"Paige, honey, are you okay?" Phoebe asked, wrapping her arms around Paige.

"Yeah, I'm fine," Paige said. "I think I'm just a little—"

"Shocked? Appalled? Confused?" Piper put in.

"Yeah. Something like that," Paige said with a small laugh.

"Listen, I really think we should discuss the idea of going to Tarsina," Leo said.

"Please don't tell me you actually think she should do this," Piper replied.

"No, not necessarily," Leo said. "But I think we should at least check it out. The Elders are shaking in their boots over this."

"They don't wear boots," Piper said, trying to lighten the moment.

"You know what I mean," Leo said. "This curse could really affect the balance between the forces of good and evil."

"And what about Paige?" Phoebe said. "She's supposed to marry some guy she just met and move to an invisible town in Switzerland?"

"I didn't say that. I said—"

"You guys!" Paige said, interrupting them. "Leo is right. We need to at least check this place out."

All the little hairs on Piper's arms stood on end. She didn't like this idea one bit. It felt a lot like her little sister was walking into a kingdom-sized trap. Or at the very least, a nightmare arranged marriage.

"Are you sure?" Piper asked her.

"Sure, I'm sure," Paige said with a determined nod.

"Okay, well, what do we do about Wyatt?" Piper asked.

"I can orb him Up There," Leo said, glancing toward the ceiling. "I'm sure the Elders wouldn't mind watching him for a while, considering the gravity of this mission."

"Fine," Piper said. Leo retrieved Wyatt from the playpen and Piper kissed his forehead. "You play nice with the ethereal beings," she told him, touching his cheek. Wyatt laughed as Phoebe and Paige kissed him too.

"We'll wait for you to get back," Paige told Leo. "We can all orb over there together."

Leo and Wyatt disappeared in a swirl of white light, and Phoebe wrapped her arms around Paige again.

"You really want to do this?" Phoebe asked, glancing across the room at Colin and Corinne, who were huddled close together on the couch.

"Yeah. If we can help them, we should help them," Paige said resignedly. "That's what we do, right? Besides, we could all use a vacation. I say we find out firsthand what this magical realm thing is all about."

Chapter Four

One moment Phoebe was standing in her warm, familiar, cozy living room. The next she was frozen to the bone and her clothes were soaked through as raindrops pelted her skin. Dark clouds loomed low overhead and wind whistled all around her, almost knocking her off her feet. She wrapped her arms around herself in a futile attempt to block the driving rain and looked through the humid, gray air at her sisters. Paige's teeth were chattering and Piper's hair was matted to her face and neck.

"Where are we?" Piper shouted to be heard over the rain.

Phoebe checked out their immediate surroundings. They were standing in a thicket of huge evergreen trees, and the mud beneath their feet was covered with a bed of wet, sticky pine needles. There wasn't a soul in sight, animal or human.

"This can't be it!" she shouted. "Shouldn't there be some kind of fairy-tale castle or something?"

"This is where Colin told me to go!" Paige said.

The others orbed in and Leo looked right up at the dark, cloudy sky. He dropped Colin's and Corinne's arms and ran over to his family, gathering them all together. Raindrops dripped from his lashes, and his dark blue shirt clung to his skin.

"Are you all right?" he asked them.

"Just a *little* wet," Piper replied.

"Where the heck is this magical kingdom of yours?" Paige shouted at Colin. "I could use some magical hot chocolate right about now."

"It's right in front of you!" Colin replied with a smile. He seemed unaffected by the rain, even though he and Corinne were as doused as Paige and her family.

"Great. A player prince with a sense of humor," Phoebe said, shaking in the cold.

"Paige, Piper, Phoebe, Leo, welcome to Tarsina!" Colin said grandly.

He lifted his arm and suddenly everything changed. Phoebe felt as if a gray veil had been lifted from her eyes. She was instantly warm and dry and her skin tingled all over with ecstatic relief. Sun poured down on her face and soothed her from the inside out. Birds twittered in the trees and a slight breeze ruffled the boughs behind her. The air was tinged with the sweet scents of fresh roses and dewy grass. But the sudden change in weather wasn't the most stunning surprise.

Right in front of her, so close that she could reach out and touch it, was a tall, white, brick wall climbing up toward the bright blue sky. The bricks gleamed so brightly in the sunlight they were almost blinding. Mouth open in awe, Phoebe placed her hand above her eyes and looked up. High, high above at the top of the wall, purple and blue flags whipped around in the wind.

"Unbelievable," Phoebe heard herself whisper.

"I don't see a gate or a door," Leo said, his eyes narrowed. "How do we get in?"

Smiling again, Colin languidly placed his hand on the wall. Beneath his fingers appeared a large wooden door with iron hinges. A medieval insignia was carved into the center of the door— a calligraphy *T* with flourishes and twists running through and around it. Phoebe, Piper, and Paige exchanged impressed glances. This was going to be interesting.

"That's the symbol you have tattooed on your arm," Paige said, reaching out to touch the etching with her fingertips.

"The symbol of my country," Colin said with a nod.

"Huh. I just thought some guy down in the Haight made it up," Paige said wryly.

Colin smiled and grasped the round handle

on the door. "Allow me," he said. Then he turned the handle and pulled.

The door let out a squeal as it swung open, as if it had been there, closed to the world, for hundreds of years. Just beyond the opening Phoebe could see a paved road and some grass, but other than that, nothing. She hesitated a split second before entering. She had seen enough traps in her life to make her naturally cautious. Who knew what they were getting themselves into? But when Corinne walked casually inside, she felt a bit better. Then Paige, ever the fearless adventurer, stepped right in after her.

"You guys coming?" she asked over her shoulder.

Phoebe shrugged. "Why not," she said, and she, Piper, and Leo followed after Paige.

"Oh . . . my . . . God," Paige said slowly, her eyes wide as she tipped her head back and looked around.

An excited, girlish grin spread across Phoebe's face. Even in her most vivid childhood daydreams, she had never imagined anything close to the reality of Tarsina. Stretching out ahead of her was a huge, wide road packed with people milling about, shopping from stalls or laughing and chatting as they strolled along the windowed shops. Placards hung from businesses advertising everything from dressmaking to perfect pies to sweetmeats. Smaller roads broke off at wild angles, crisscrossing their way between white brick buildings of all shapes and sizes. Flags danced on every rooftop, and many of the windows boasted banners with intricate designs in bright, regal colors. The flourishing *T* seemed to be everywhere.

"Wow," Phoebe said. "This is like—"

"A real fairy tale," Piper finished.

Somewhere nearby a horse let out a whinny and a bunch of kids laughed. Phoebe could hear hooves clomping against stone and the creak of a wagon's wheels. Fifteen feet away a woman bartered with an elderly man for a box of brown and white eggs. A couple of little girls in beribboned dresses scampered by, rolling a hoop with a stick and giggling all the way. It was almost impossible for Phoebe to believe that she wasn't dreaming.

"Pretty cool, isn't it?" Corinne said, tying her blond hair back from her face.

"That would be a severe understatement," Phoebe replied.

"Come on. We'll walk up Kingston Road to the palace," Colin said, leading the way into the busy street in front of them.

"Did I really just hear someone say we're going to walk up to the palace?" Paige said, leaning in toward Phoebe's ear.

"I know!" Phoebe replied giddily. "This is so surreal."

The sisters and Leo all kept close together as they walked, looking around as if they were in a living museum display. At first it seemed like all the women had stepped right out of medieval times in their full skirts and scarved heads. But every now and then Phoebe caught a glimpse of a young woman dressed in khakis and a T-shirt or a guy in faded denim and Doc Martens. A woman in a silken gown stepped up to a vegetable vendor who wore a Grateful Dead T-shirt and love beads. The little boy at her heels, while dressed in a vest and knickers, was intent on his beeping, bleeping Game Boy.

"I guess these are the modern influences they were talking about," Piper said, tilting her head toward a bright yellow Hummer parked next to the tailor's.

"Check it out. Satellite," Paige said, pointing up.

Sure enough, three satellite dishes sat atop a high, slated turret, cupped toward the sky. Just below them, hanging in a rounded window, was a red and blue Red Sox pennant.

"The Red Sox?" Leo asked. "As in the Boston Red Sox?"

"Oh, the people of Tarsina *love* the Red Sox," Corinne said with a smile.

"The team was cursed just like our kingdom," Colin explained. "The people of Tarsina can relate. And we were all so thrilled when they won the Series. . . ."

Phoebe snorted a laugh and Piper shook her head. This place was full of surprises.

"Prince Colin!" an elderly woman gasped, instantly dropping into a low bow. She wiped her hands vigorously on her apron as if she was afraid Colin might be offended by the grime.

A murmur went through the crowd, and all around them people stopped what they were doing and dropped their heads. Phoebe, Piper, Paige, and Leo paused in the sudden silence. They were the tallest people on the crowded street now, looking down at the backs of all those bent heads.

"Please! Everyone! Go back to your business!" Colin shouted, raising his hands. "I'm merely showing my new friends around town."

Slowly everything picked up again, but a few people bowed once more before casting curious glances over the prince's friends and then getting back to work. A little girl ran up to Paige, blond curls bouncing around her face.

"Are you her? Are you going to be the princess and save the kingdom?" she asked Paige, her blue eyes full of hope.

Paige's heart dropped, and she looked at Colin.

"Uh . . . we'll see about that, sweetie," she said, crouching down in front of her.

"Diana! Come back here!"

The little girl's mother broke away from the crowded sidewalk and scooped her daughter up in her arms.

"I'm so sorry," she said, holding the girl to

her. "She's very rambunctious. I apologize if she bothered you, Your Eminence," she said, dropping a quick curtsy to Colin.

"She was no bother," Colin replied with a quick, but somehow sad, smile. He reached out and ran his hand over the girl's curls and she blushed, burying her face in her mother's chest. "She's beautiful."

"Thank you, Your Highness," the woman said, flushing with pleasure. Then she cast her own hopeful glance at all three sisters, bowed once more, and carried her daughter back down the road.

"You see, they're all watching us, wondering," Colin said as they started to move again. "They all know that my birthday is coming. They're all counting on me to save them. I'm sure they take the arrival of strangers as a sign that I'm working toward a solution. I'm sure they're wondering where you came from, and who you are."

Phoebe could feel the uneasiness that permeated the streets, and it made her stomach flutter with queasy butterflies. Her empathic powers gave her the ability to feel the emotions that those around her were feeling. Sometimes it was great, like when everyone had first bowed to Colin and she could feel the love of his people pouring out of them. But the furtive expectation around her now just made her feel worried and nauseous. Her heart went out to these people who were clearly fearing for their lives and the lives of their children. The citizens of Tarsina took this curse very seriously.

"They're all so scared," Phoebe said under her breath to Piper.

"If what Colin told us is true, they have every right to be," Piper replied, smiling reassuringly at a couple of little boys who were gaping up at them.

Phoebe followed her sister's lead and smiled around at the people, trying to put them at ease. She received some smiles in return, and a few women even curtsied as they moved up the street. Phoebe felt like she was part of a very small parade and everyone had come out to see her.

"It's like we're famous," Paige said.

"Nah. We're just strangers who happen to be walking next to the famous guy," Piper replied.

Phoebe caught the eye of an older man, all dressed in black, staring at her from the side of the road. She gave him a smile, but he just glared back with a hard, weathered face. His ice blue eyes narrowed the longer she stared at him, and Phoebe felt a cold chill slice right through her. The force of it knocked the wind right out of her, and she shivered and grabbed Piper's arm.

"Phoebe? What is it?" Piper asked, supporting her with both hands.

"That man," Phoebe said, catching her breath. "There was so much hatred coming off him. And it felt like . . . it felt like it was directed at us."

"What man?" Leo asked, scanning the crowd.

Phoebe looked at the spot where the man in black had been standing, but there was no one there.

"He's gone," she said, swallowing hard. Her veins still throbbed from the reverberations of his hate.

"It must have been a loyalist," Colin said, scanning the crowd intently.

"A loyalist?" Piper asked.

"Yes. There are some living among us who are loyal to the curse," Colin explained. "They don't want me to marry. They want the curse to come true."

"And for all those people to die?" Phoebe asked.

Colin nodded solemnly. "Leaving only pure magical Tarsinians behind."

"That's just evil," Paige said.

"Yes, it is evil, but it's our reality. The loyalist tradition dates back to before the curse was ever cast," Colin told them, his face grim. "Come. We've got some more ground to cover." He turned and started up the road again with Corinne and Paige on either side.

"Are you okay?" Leo asked, his hand supporting Phoebe's back.

"Yeah. I'm fine," Phoebe said, glancing around as she steadied herself. "I'll be fine. As long as I don't have to feel that again."

As she, Piper, and Leo hastened to catch up

with the others, Phoebe cast a glance over her shoulder, trying to find the man in the throng. This place was so gorgeous and peaceful and full of love, it was hard to believe someone that cold and hollowed out by hate could exist here. But for the first time since stepping through the door into Tarsina, Phoebe could believe that dark mystical forces could be gathering here. A few guys like that, backed up by an ancient curse? The kingdom wouldn't stand a chance.

"There it is," Colin said as the little group of travelers came to the top of Kingston Road. "Home sweet home."

About half a mile away, across another wide street and past a border of immaculately kept gardens that were bursting with red and purple flowers, a huge castle rose up toward the sky. Paige gazed up at the palace walls, her heart fluttering in excitement. Turrets and towers loomed above, their incredible height topped only by the snow-capped mountains of the Alps around them. Guards patrolled the highest points, gazing down at the street below. A maid popped out of one window, beating a large, crimson rug with a cloth-covered stick. A lake of clear blue water surrounded the palace, and it took Paige a moment to realize that she was looking at a moat. An actual moat.

"This is insane," she said under her breath.

"You think that's insane? Check this out," Piper said, gazing down the street.

Paige's eyes widened as a beautiful gilded coach, drawn by four prancing white horses, careened around a corner. The driver was dressed in velvet and silk, a feather plume adorning his puffy black hat. The horses whinnied as he pulled the reins up tight and brought the carriage to a halt right in front of the prince.

"Welcome back, Your Majesty," the driver said, tipping his hat.

"Thank you, Jonathan," Colin said, nodding. A footman jumped off the back of the coach and ran around to open the door for them.

"Ladies?" Colin said. "After you."

"Where did this thing come from?" Paige asked as Phoebe climbed into the coach ahead of them.

"The lookouts send for my horses when they see me coming," Colin told her. "I've never entered the palace on foot in my life. It's just not done."

"Ah. Why do I get the feeling that there are a lot of things that are just not done around here?" Paige said.

Colin flushed and looked at his feet. "You know what it's like to have to live within a set of rules," he said, holding out his hand to help her into the coach.

"I do," she replied. "That's why we're constantly breaking them."

She raised one eyebrow at him as she stepped inside and joined her sisters and Leo. There was no doubt in her mind that if Colin broke his particular rules, the consequences could be much greater than anything she and her sisters had ever lived through, but sometimes you had to try. Piper and Leo had married even though it was against the rules, and they had suffered for it, but it had turned out great in the end. And she couldn't count how many times she and her sisters had gone up against the Elders or some mystical council and convinced them that their way was the best way. How hard had Colin and Corinne actually tried?

"Well, this is where I get off," Corinne said, looking up at them from the ground.

"You're not coming to the palace?" Paige asked, leaning through the window.

"You're about to meet your new parents-in-law," Corinne said, her eyes full of sadness. "I don't think it would be appropriate for me to be there."

Paige's heart went out to Corinne. This was beyond unfair. She vowed right then and there that she would play along for now, but if there was anything she could do to help Corinne and Colin be together, she would do it. There had to be something the two of them had overlooked.

"We'll see you soon," she promised Corinne. Then she turned away to give Colin and his love some privacy while they said good-bye.

Finally Colin climbed into the coach and the footman slammed the door, latching it shut. The horses lurched forward, and Corinne lifted her hand in a wave as Paige and the others were whisked off to the castle. Paige stared out the window, taking it all in as the coach rumbled over the drawbridge and through the castle gates. She still couldn't believe that a place like this actually existed, let alone that she was really there.

Suddenly Colin's eyes brightened and he sat up straight in his seat. "My father's come to meet us."

Paige looked out the far window and got her first glimpse of the king of Tarsina. He was standing in front of a huge door with servants lined up on either side of him, each standing at perfect attention. He was an older, jovial-looking man with white hair and a close-cropped beard. Although he was clearly well into his golden years, there wasn't a stoop or a slouch about him. He stood straight, tall, and strong, his eyes shining and his mouth lifted in a happy grin. When the coach stopped, he lifted his arms wide to accept his son.

Colin hopped down from the coach and embraced his father. "King Philip of Tarsina," he said. "I'd like you to meet my potential bride, Paige Matthews."

Paige glanced at her sisters and lifted her eyebrows before descending from the coach. At least Colin had called her a "potential" bride. Nothing had been decided . . . yet.

"Paige! Welcome to Tarsina!" King Philip said, his voice booming as he wrapped Paige up in a hug. He held her out at arm's length, his soft hands gently holding hers. "Let me look at you," he said, then he smiled at Colin. "I think she'll fit right in."

"Thank you," Paige said, wondering what, exactly, would be an appropriate way to greet a royal. "You have a lovely . . . kingdom."

King Philip let out a loud laugh and slapped Colin on the back, then brought them both to him in the crooks of his arms. "Come. You must meet the queen."

Just then he noticed Phoebe, Piper, and Leo stepping down from the coach. "And who do we have here?" he asked, releasing Colin and Paige.

"These are my sisters, Phoebe and Piper," Paige said. "And this is Piper's husband, Leo."

"Hello, Your Majesty," Piper said. "It's a pleasure to meet you."

King Philip's eyes widened slightly and he bowed his head. "The Charmed Ones. All three of you. In my palace," he said, his mouth set in a reverential smile. "It's an honor."

Piper, Paige, and Phoebe exchanged shocked looks. They were famous in a land they hadn't even known existed. How very cool.

"The honor is ours," Phoebe said finally, recovering herself.

"I thank you. Let us go inside," King Philip said, clapping his hands together and reclaiming his casual demeanor. "The queen will never believe we've got all of you here."

As the king led them through a huge open-air atrium and into the wide tapestry-lined hallway behind, he and Colin fell into an easy conversation about the prince's adventures in America. Paige dropped back to walk with her sisters and Leo, taking in the torches that lit the walls and the paintings of former kings.

"Can you believe this place?" Piper asked as they passed by a room guarded by two statue-like sentries.

"At least the king seems nice," Paige said.

"It's not the king you have to worry about," Phoebe replied under her breath. "It's the queen. It's always the queen."

The group came to a large wooden door, and two men jumped to attention to open it for the king and his son. They stepped into a large chamber lit by the bright sun streaming in through dozens of huge windows. People milled about, talking in hushed tones or listening to the music being played by a flutist in the near corner. At the far end of the room stood four thrones, two large and ornate, the other two slightly simpler. A tall woman sat in one of the large thrones, smiling placidly as a pair of maids presented various linens for her approval.

"My dear, our son has returned and he has

brought with him a bride," the king announced.

"Potential bride," Paige amended quietly. But the king did not correct himself.

The queen looked up and dismissed the maids with a wave of her hand. Paige expected her to rise and walk over to them, but instead she flicked her fingers at her husband, and he cleared his throat before leading them all forward. Paige's heart thumped with foreboding.

"What did I tell you?" Phoebe said through her teeth.

"You know your fairy tales, sister," Paige replied wryly.

As they stepped closer to the queen, her intense beauty became more and more clear. She was younger than her husband by at least ten years. Her blond hair was pulled back tightly from her face, accentuating her high cheekbones and piercing blue eyes. She wore heavy, diva-style makeup and a bodice that accentuated a tiny waist. Her dress was made entirely of thick, purple brocade with gold piping along the seams. She would have been breathtaking if there wasn't such a hard, cold quality about her.

"Which one of you is to be my son's wife?" she asked, her gaze falling on Piper.

"Don't look at me," Piper said, reaching for Leo's hand. "I'm taken."

The queen's cold eyes flicked over Leo, dismissing him like he was a speck of dust. They settled on Phoebe for only a moment before traveling on to Paige. She glanced at her sisters before meeting the queen's gaze head-on. Inside, her heart was pounding with nervousness, which irritated her. Paige wasn't easily intimidated by people, and she didn't see why Colin's mom should be any different. She lifted her chin and tried to look cool and collected.

"Mother, this is Paige Matthews," Colin said, taking Paige's hand and urging her to step forward. "She has agreed to come to Tarsina and consider my offer. Paige, my mother, Queen Ramona of Tarsina."

The queen's severely plucked eyebrows arched. "*Consider* his offer? Is my son not good enough for you?"

"Yes. Of course he is," Paige said. "I thought I should see where I would be living and meet your people before making a decision about the rest of my life . . . Your Highness."

The queen narrowed her eyes for a moment and then nodded curtly. "Shrewd girl," she said. "I like that."

Paige shot her sisters a triumphant glance. So much for scary mothers-in-law.

The queen stood, lifted a large gold necklace with a single red stone at the center from around her own neck, and held it out to Paige.

"What's that?" Paige asked.

"This is the queen's rune," Colin explained. "The necklace is passed on from the reigning queen to the new princess upon her engagement."

"I realize you are just *considering* at this time, my dear, but my people need to see that Colin is engaged," the queen said. "They need some peace. If you decide not to accept his offer of marriage, you may always return the rune."

Paige swallowed hard, looking at the shining stone. Tales of cursed jewels danced through her head. As a witch, accepting jewelry from strangers was as dangerous as taking candy from them would be for a child. But she trusted that Colin wouldn't do anything to hurt her, and when he nodded at her to take it, she bowed her head toward the queen.

The cold necklace slipped over Paige's head and settled heavily around her neck. She reached up and touched the rune and smiled at the queen.

"Thank you," she said sincerely.

"Welcome to our home," the queen said with a short smile. She looked up at the others and the smile widened slightly. "All of you . . . welcome."

Then, before anyone could reply, the queen snapped her fingers to summon her maids back to her side and sat down on her throne again. Paige glanced at Colin uncertainly, and the king swept his arm around her shoulders and turned her away from the queen.

"Don't mind my wife," he said. "She's very distracted, what with the ball we'll be throwing in your honor this evening."

"A ball?" Piper said. "Shouldn't you be saving the ball for the girl that Colin is actually going to marry?"

"Piper," Paige said through her teeth.

"What? Nothing's been decided yet, has it?" Piper said. "I just don't want the king to go to all this trouble if we might be going back to San Francisco tomorrow," she added with a little too much sweetness. Paige knew that her sister was treating all of this as some kind of game. It was impossible for Piper to conceive of breaking up the family. In her mind, they *were* all going back to San Francisco tomorrow. Paige, however, was not so sure. She still had a lot to think about.

She looked at Colin and the king. "So is it really true, King Philip?" she asked. "If Colin doesn't marry by Wednesday, those people we met out there on the street, the people in this room . . . ?"

The king's kind face turned grim and he nodded sadly. "It's true. Many of them are doomed to die if Colin does not marry a pure magical being," he said. "I don't mean to pressure you, my dear, but you may be our only hope."

"Yeah, no pressure there," Phoebe said quietly.

"I'm only trying to tell the truth," King Philip said. "What you do with it is up to you."

Paige took a deep breath as a couple of children skipped by and ran around the flutist's legs. By the window a pair of clearly smitten

eenagers flirted and kissed. An elderly woman
sat next to them, a placid smile on her face as she
listened to the music. Paige couldn't imagine
that at this time next week many of these people
could just be gone.

She looked at the king and squared her shoulders. "Let's talk about this ball."

Chapter Five

"This will be your room for the duration of your stay here with us," Colin said, spreading his arms wide in the center of the cavernous chamber. "The princess's quarters are, of course, much larger."

"Larger than this?" Paige said, as Phoebe let out an impressed whistle.

The entire first floor of the manor could have fit within the walls of the sprawling room. Wooden beams crossed the vaulted ceilings and drapes of silk hung from the walls, framing the massive four-poster bed. There were couches and pillows strewn everywhere for lounging, and a dressing area in the corner boasted a vanity table and a full-length, three-view mirror. Hanging on a rack next to the table were fifteen stunningly gorgeous ball gowns that had been sent for the three women.

I could get used to this, Paige thought, raising her eyebrows.

"Paige, you have to know that if you do con-
sent to marry me, I will do everything in my
power to help you continue to live your life the
way you want to live it," Colin said. He
stepped forward, took both her hands in his,
and looked deep into her eyes. "You won't even
have to live here. With your orbing power, you
could merely come back for official functions
and holidays."

"Is that the life you really want?" Paige asked
him gently. "A life with a wife who doesn't even
live with you?"

"This isn't about what I want," Colin said, his
expression determined. "It's about my duty. And
I have a feeling that you and I could make it
work," he added with a small smile.

Paige looked around, considering the offer.
The place was amazing, and Colin was an
incredible man. The sacrifices he was willing to
make for his people left her almost breathless.
She knew what she would be giving up if she
agreed to marry him, but it wasn't like she had a
boyfriend or even a potential boyfriend to think
of. Maybe she could actually—

"And, of course, we would have to produce
an heir," Colin said suddenly.

Paige's heart dropped to the stone floor.
"What?" she asked, automatically withdrawing
her hands. "An heir? You mean a . . . a baby?"

"Oh, not right away!" Colin amended
quickly. "But in the next couple of years or so."

"I think I need to sit down," Paige said, taking a couple of steps back. Leo jumped forward and sat her down on the edge of the bed.

A baby? she thought, her mind reeling. She wanted children, of course. Being around Wyatt had definitely sparked a maternal instinct within her. But sometime in the next two years? That was not part of her life's plan.

"Paige? Are you all right?" Colin asked.

"Sure. Just a little . . . warm," Paige said. "Is there any water around here?"

"I'll fetch your handmaiden," Colin said.

"No. Don't worry about it," Piper said. "Maybe you should just leave us alone for a little while. We have some things to talk about."

Colin glanced at Paige and looked as if he wanted to say something, but then thought better of it. Instead he bowed and quickly walked out. Paige flopped back on the cushy bed and brought her hand to her forehead.

Princess Paige with a baby on the way.

And to think, a few days ago all she had to think about was a few Ping-Pong balls.

"All right, that's it. I'm nipping this in the bud!" Piper announced, throwing her hands up. "Paige, you cannot do this."

She stood in front of Paige and watched as her younger sister sat up on the bed. Even though Paige's face was all blotchy and red and she was clearly reeling, she fixed an intent stare on Piper.

"Why not? I mean . . . of course we'll have to produce an heir," Paige said. "It's the royal family, right? They're all *about* producing the next ruler of the country. I hadn't thought of it before, but—better to know now . . . right?"

"Forget about the baby thing. I'm not talking about the baby thing," Piper ranted. "I'm talking about you losing out on the chance to marry for love. Why are you so eager to sell yourself short like this?"

"She's right, sweetie," Phoebe said, sitting down next to Paige. She smoothed Paige's hair behind her ear and held her hand. "If you do this, you're giving up so many possibilities."

"And besides, look at you!" Piper pointed out. "You practically fainted when he mentioned having a kid. You're not ready to be a wife, let alone a mother."

Much to Piper's relief, Paige slowly started to nod. She gripped Phoebe's hand and stood up, looking stronger by the second.

"You're right," she said. "I can't marry a random stranger. I can't have his baby. What about . . . what about Corinne? The poor girl is heartbroken."

"I hate to point out the obvious, but if you don't go through with this, thousands of people will die," Leo said.

"Leo!" Piper said, her frustration bursting out of her.

"What? I'm sorry. I'm just telling it like it is,"

Leo said, throwing his hands out. "Do you think I want Paige to be pressured into a marriage she doesn't want? Of course I don't. But I don't want thousands of deaths hanging over our heads either."

"He's right," Phoebe said quietly. "We have to do something."

Paige let out a little groan and looked from Phoebe to Piper. Piper read the look in her little sister's eyes. She needed help, and Piper had no idea how she was going to do it, but she was going to help her.

"We have to find some of these people who are loyal to the curse," Piper said finally.

"The who what?" Phoebe asked.

"The loyalists, remember?" Piper said. "If there are people here who are so gung ho to have this curse come true, then they probably know more about it than anyone. Maybe they know of a loophole."

"She's right," Leo said. "They might be protecting some secret. Some way to break the curse."

There was a light rap on the door and a pretty young girl, about fifteen years old, stuck her head in. She was wearing a white cap and her red hair was pulled back in a thick braid.

"I'm sorry to bother you, miss, but we were sent to help you and your sisters get dressed for the ball," she said, biting her lip.

Paige sighed. "Okay. Come in."

The girl entered, followed by a troop of women who all walked over to the dressing area and started to bustle about. Piper watched as they fluffed crinolines and laid out various makeup brushes.

"Now's our chance," Piper said, lowering her voice. "Paige, you and Leo go to the ball. Phoebe and I will hit the streets and see if we can find some of the bad guys."

"The streets? Oh, but I want to wear one of the pretty dresses," Phoebe whimpered.

"You want to play dress-up or save our sister?" Piper asked her.

"All right," Phoebe said with mock resignation, earning a whack on the arm from Paige.

"Lady Paige?" one of the maids called. "We should get started."

"Lady Paige? Weird," Paige said.

"Okay, go primp," Piper said to Paige. "Distract them and we'll sneak out."

"Got it," Paige said with a nod. She shook her hair back and walked over to the ten women bustling about in the corner. "Who wants to dress the future princess of Tarsina?" she called out, eliciting a gasp of awe and a few giggles as everyone rushed to volunteer.

"Good luck," Leo told Phoebe and Piper. "And watch your backs."

"We always do," Piper said. Leo smiled and left.

Then Piper and Phoebe slipped out the door as Paige slipped into an exquisite blue gown.

The sun was just setting behind the great wall around the kingdom as Phoebe and Piper stepped out onto one of the main streets of Tarsina. Phoebe pulled the hood of the black cloak she was wearing up over her head. She and Piper had swiped them from a coatroom near the door, wanting to disguise themselves in case anyone recognized them from Kingston Road that morning. It would be difficult to get the loyalists to trust them if they knew that Phoebe and Piper were the Charmed sisters of the future princess. Piper had also pointed out that loyalists who hated people from the outside world most likely didn't dress in jeans and halter tops.

"So, where are we going?" Piper asked, stepping up onto the sidewalk.

"I don't know. This is your plan," Phoebe reminded her.

They rounded a corner and found themselves in the midst of a crowded street fair. Booths lined the road, strung with little flags and signs advertising games to play and sweets for sale. Kids ran around, clutching balloons and stuffing their faces with cotton candy. A pair of boys blew by Phoebe, nearly knocking her off her feet.

"Tristan! Michael! Stop! Stop right there!" their mother called after them. "Ooh! If you don't stop!"

Finally she lifted her hands in frustration and opened them toward the running boys. Instantly, they froze in their tracks, their mouths open in laughter, their feet suspended in the air. Phoebe's heart practically stopped in her chest. The woman was practicing magic right there on the street! Everyone was going to see!

"Sorry about that," the woman said, lifting her long skirt as she stepped past Phoebe. "My boys have no manners."

"That's . . . that's okay," Phoebe said, her pulse starting to flow again.

She cracked a laugh and looked at Piper as the woman grabbed her kids by the backs of their shirts and they started moving again, squirming in their mother's grasp. The people around them just kept going about their business as if nothing had happened. No one was gasping in disbelief or running in fear.

"Crazy, huh?" Piper said with a wry smile. "Check out this guy."

She pointed at a man selling roasted peanuts across the street. He lit the fire under one of the trays . . . with his finger. Another group of kids chased a younger boy, tossing pebbles at him and teasing him. The little boy raced behind a garbage can and suddenly shrank down to the size of a mouse. He hid inside a discarded popcorn box until the other boys trotted by. Then he restored himself to his normal height and ran off in the opposite direction.

"Wow. Maybe Paige *should* come to live here," Phoebe said as she and Piper started walking again. "Maybe we should *all* come to live here."

"Phoebe—"

"No! Just imagine it! We could use our powers right out here in the open and no one would even bat an eyelash," Phoebe said, her heart feeling fit to burst. "Just imagine the freedom, Piper! We would never have to worry about being exposed. Ever!"

"Mommy! My balloon!" a little girl shouted nearby.

Phoebe saw the girl pointing toward the sky and caught sight of a fat red balloon, slowly making its way into the atmosphere. She grinned at Piper, then levitated up and grabbed the string. Phoebe felt as light as air in more ways than one. It was so incredibly freeing, using her powers in front of everyone.

"Here you go," she said, handing the balloon over as she returned to the ground.

"Thanks," the girl said with a smile.

No scared tears, no expression of shock. Just a "Thanks."

The girl's mother smiled at Phoebe, and then the little family disappeared into the crowd.

"How cool was that?" Phoebe said giddily.

"Very cool," Piper said with a nod and a smile. "Now come on, Supergirl, we've got more to save around here than balloons."

Phoebe and Piper walked to the end of the

block and out of the street fair. The sky was darkening rapidly. All around them, flames appeared in the old-fashioned streetlamps, sparked magically to life on some invisible timer. At the corner Piper and Phoebe paused to check out the various streets.

"Okay, if you were an evil loyalist, where would you hang out?" Piper asked.

Phoebe gazed down the street to her left, a shiver running over her skin. A few doors down she noticed a dark sign with gold lettering. A couple of men in black cloaks opened the door beneath the sign and glanced around before they slunk inside. Their paranoid demeanor screamed "guilty."

"St. John's Pub looks promising," Phoebe said, pointing down the street. "Not exactly an upbeat clientele."

"Looks good to me," Piper said, pulling her cloak more tightly around her. "Let's go."

One glance through the grime-smeared windows and Phoebe knew her instinct had been correct. The tiny bar was packed with men and women in dark clothing, huddled around low wooden tables, their faces lit only by sparse candlelight. A bar lined the right wall and people slumped on the stools, nursing their brews. There was nothing festive or light about the place.

"You ready, sis?" Piper asked, tilting her head toward the door.

Phoebe took a deep breath. She had a feeling she was going to get hit with some intense emotion in this place. She was going to have to be on her guard.

"Ready," she replied.

Piper pushed through the door and made her way over to an empty table in the center of the room. Phoebe would have felt more comfortable hiding out in a corner, but she knew why her sister had chosen this spot. All kinds of people surrounded them, talking and whispering and snickering. If they were going to learn anything, this would be the place to learn it.

"What can I getcha?" a barmaid asked, the wide neck of her dress tumbling off her shoulder.

Phoebe looked around. This didn't seem like the type of place where you ordered cosmopolitans. "Two beers," she said.

"You got it," the woman told them, moving away.

"Didja see the new princess?" a guy at the next table asked, his voice low and scratchy. "She's beautiful. Even for Colin."

Phoebe glanced at Piper and smiled. Paige already had some admirers.

"You know how those women from outside like ta party," another man said. A suggestive laugh went up around the table, and the men all clinked glasses before downing their brews.

Phoebe's jaw dropped. It was all she could do

to keep from getting in the guy's face and defending her sister. Piper put a calming hand on Phoebe's knee under the table. They couldn't exactly take on an entire bar full of magical beings. Well, they could, but it wasn't worth it.

"Looks like he's gonna do it," a wiry man at another table said. "He's found himself a Charmed One. Doesn't get more purely magical than that."

"So much for the curse," the woman on his lap put in.

"Not so fast," the large guy sitting across from them said. "It's not a done deal. We could still get 'em to call off the wedding."

"How?"

"I say we focus on her," the man suggested, leaning his beefy arms on the table. "She ain't from around here. I bet she'll scare off real easy."

I don't like the sound of that, Phoebe thought. Her stomach tightened and she looked at Piper. Clearly they had come to the right place.

"How're we supposed to get to her, though?" the wiry man asked.

"Yeah, she's livin' in the palace," his woman added. "She's gonna be surrounded by guards all the time."

"Well, it's not like we haven't gotten into the palace before. Right, my friends?" the beefy man said with a triumphant leer. "We can do it again."

Phoebe's heart was pounding now. These

people did not mess around. If they had gotten into the palace before, who was to say that Paige wasn't in danger right now?

"We have to talk to Sinjin," the wiry man said. "Sinjin probably already has a plan."

"Sinjin always has a plan," the woman agreed.

"To Sinjin!" the beefy man called out.

Everyone in the pub raised their glasses and called out, "To Sinjin!"

Phoebe leaned in toward her sister. "Guess we're looking for Sinjin, then?"

"Seems that way," Piper replied.

Just then, two huge mugs of beer were slapped down on the table in front of them. Phoebe and Piper sprang apart and looked up at the barmaid. Her watery eyes slid from Piper to Phoebe and back again, and she crossed her arms over her ample chest.

"You know, I been thinking about it, and I don't think I've seen you two around here before," she said.

The people at the adjacent tables fell silent and looked at Phoebe and Piper. Phoebe's heart nearly pounded out of her chest, but she kept her cool. After years of confrontations with the most frightening beings on Earth and in the underworld, she had pretty much perfected this talent. But her initial anxiety soon turned to anger. Who were these people to sit around and talk about hurting Paige?

"A girl can't come in for a drink?" Phoebe asked, looking the woman in the eye.

"Sinjin don't like strangers coming in here," a gruff old man behind Piper said, spilling half his beer on the table as he lifted it. "Doesn't trust 'em."

"Well maybe we should meet this Sinjin, then," Piper said, her veneer as smooth as Phoebe's. "Then we won't be strangers."

"He's not here," the waitress replied. "And I think you two might want to not be here as well." She picked up their drinks again and took a step back to give them room to get out.

Phoebe looked at Piper, her eyes wide. There wasn't much they could do with dozens of angry strangers staring them down.

"We'll be back," Piper said finally, standing up.

"Yeah, that's what I thought you'd say," the barmaid told them.

As Phoebe and Piper made a beeline for the door, Phoebe kept expecting a fireball or some other magical weapon to explode next to her face, but nothing came. The second the door was closed behind them, a laugh went up all across the bar. Apparently the loyalists didn't see two little witches as a potential threat.

"They think we're a joke," Piper said, clearly offended.

Phoebe hooked her arm through her sister's and started up the road. "Yeah, well, they have no idea who they're dealing with."

• • •

Paige twirled around the dance floor in Colin's arms, the skirts of her dress fanning out around her. The faces of the crowd were a blur as she spun by, but she could tell that everyone was smiling as they gazed upon her and Colin. They couldn't take their eyes off the royal couple. She was a tremendous hit.

"Are you having fun?" Colin asked, holding her close as they waltzed.

"Actually, I am," she said, grinning. "I don't even know how I'm doing this. I never learned how to dance."

"The ballroom is enchanted," Colin said. "Everyone who walks through those doors becomes an expert dancer."

Paige nodded, impressed. "Nice touch. I'd like to put a spell like that on P3."

"It's an easy charm," Colin told her. "Remind me to teach you."

"I will," Paige said.

The song came to a close and Colin twirled her one last time, then lowered her into a beautiful, low dip. Paige's smile widened as the room erupted in applause. Colin helped her up and they both lifted their hands to acknowledge their admirers, then he led her off the dance floor.

"We're so glad you're here," a woman in a high-necked dress said to Paige as they passed.

"You're our savior," another man said.

"Long live Princess Paige!" a younger man

shouted, causing a round of hearty cheers.

Paige felt her face flush and her heart turned in her chest. Part of her was thrilled at the excitement of it all and at the possibility that she could, truly, save these people from a horrible fate. Another part of her felt like a sham. She felt guilty and horrible and dishonest. These people had all pinned their hopes on her and she felt she was not worthy. After all, she was still considering turning Colin down. She didn't deserve their love.

"You look like you could use some air," Colin said, leading her toward a pair of huge glass doors.

Two guards opened the doors for the couple, and Paige stepped out onto a large verandah overlooking the expansive rose garden behind the castle. She stepped to the marble railing and took a long, deep breath.

"Are you all right? Can I get you anything?" Colin asked her gently.

"No. I'm fine," Paige said, happy to be away from the hundreds of expectant, hopeful faces. "Colin . . . I just don't know if I can do this."

Colin's face paled slightly, but he nodded. "I understand."

Paige swallowed against the thickness that welled up in her throat. Her eyes stung with hot, sorrowful tears. She hated the position he had put her in. It was either give up her life, or give up the lives of thousands of others.

"I understand, Paige. I do," Colin went on. "You're scared. You can't imagine a future away from the life you know. But I . . . I can't imagine a future in this kingdom knowing I could have saved half my people but failed."

"Colin—"

"You're a protector of the innocent," Colin said. "We both are. It's what we were born to do. You know what your destiny has always been. All I'm asking you to do is add to it. You have a chance here to be a hero to my people. You have a chance to save an entire kingdom."

Paige took a deep breath. Suddenly the tears were subsiding.

"I know this place doesn't seem real to you. None of this seems real," Colin continued desperately. "But it's real to me. Until recently, it's all I've ever known. Just think, if this were San Francisco—if it was either marry me or half the people of San Francisco would die—what would you do?"

Paige's heart flipped over and she looked at Colin. Now *his* eyes were swimming in tears. He loved his people so much, this whole thing was clearly tearing him apart. It was tearing an entire population apart.

"I know it's not a perfect offer. I know it's not an offer of true love, but I will always care for you and respect you and be a true husband," Colin said. "Come on, am I really that bad?" he asked with a bit of a smile.

Paige let out a laugh that sounded more like a cry. "No. You're not really that bad," she said, her vision swimming once again.

Colin looked at her uncertainly but took a deep and bracing breath. "Then I'm going to ask you one more time, and I promise, this will be the last."

He pulled the engagement ring out of his pocket and got down on one knee before her. Tears streamed down Paige's cheeks, and she was unable to tell whether they were tears of sorrow or joy or regret or pride.

"Paige Matthews, will you marry me?" Colin asked, his eyes clear with hope. "Will you be my princess?"

Paige nodded and crouched down in front of him to look straight into his eyes. "Yes, Colin," she said determinedly. "Yes, I will."

Chapter Six

"Hi! You told us to come back in the morning, so here we are," Piper said, stalking up to the guard in front of Paige's bedroom door. "So are you going to let us in to see our sister now?"

Piper was so tired she felt as if she had walked around all night with six bags of flour strapped to her arms and legs. Her eyes were so dry they stung, and she wasn't entirely certain she was thinking clearly. She hadn't seen her little sister since dusk the day before, and after a sleepless night, she was hovering on the brink of a panic attack.

All this thanks to the guard who now stood before her with crumbs in his wiry black beard, the morning sun glinting off his silver headgear.

"There's no reason to be upset with me," the guard said in his infuriatingly patient tone. "I told you, it was Lady Paige herself who gave me the orders. She didn't wish to be disturbed."

"Well, we'd like to disturb her now, all right, buddy?" Phoebe said, glaring up at him. "Is *Lady Paige* up yet?"

The guard, who towered over Piper and Phoebe, smirked. "The maid just brought in her breakfast. You may enter now."

"Gee, thanks," Phoebe said, narrowing her eyes as he opened the door for them.

Piper slipped inside and let out a huge sigh of relief when she saw that Paige was safe and sound, sitting up in bed with a tray before her. She was surrounded by plush satin pillows and sheets and looked as rested as a princess should look. She was wearing a beautiful pink nightgown with white lace all along the plunging neckline. The queen's rune around her neck sparkled in the sunshine that streamed through the windows. Paige had woken up in a fairy tale, while Piper had spent a restless night fretting for her sister's safety. Five seconds after her relief registered, Piper was back to being annoyed.

"Paige! What were you thinking ordering the guards to keep us out of your room last night?" Piper blurted, storming over to the bedside.

Paige took a bite of her eggs Benedict and twisted her lips into a wry pucker. "Good morning to you, too, Piper."

"You know what we went out to do last night," Piper replied. Her stomach grumbled as she looked over Paige's breakfast spread, but she ignored it. "Didn't you think we'd want to share?"

"Well if you wanted to get in here so badly, why didn't you just freeze the guards?" Paige asked.

"Everyone's a good witch around here," Piper semi-whined. "I can't freeze anyone. And you know what? I shouldn't have to. I should be able to get into my own sister's bedroom."

Phoebe plopped onto the bed next to Paige, stole a piece of toast, and crunched into it. Piper had to struggle to keep from rolling her eyes. Was she the only person around here who realized the gravity of the situation?

"Look, I didn't specifically order them to keep you out," Paige said, taking another bite. "I just told them I didn't want to be disturbed. It was a long ball. I was tired."

"Oooh, tell us about the ball," Phoebe said, cuddling up next to Paige. "Were there tons of beautiful dresses? Any hot guys? What did the queen wear?"

"Phoebe!" Piper scolded.

"Piper, chill out a little," Paige said. "Take a load off. Have some breakfast. The fruit here is like nothing you've ever tasted before."

Piper tipped her head back, sighed, and finally gave up. She sat down at Paige's feet, leaned over, and grabbed a slice of melon from her tray. One bite and the sweet taste exploded in her mouth, the cool juice slipping down her throat.

"Wow," she said, her mouth full. "You're not kidding."

"Ya see?" Paige said with a nod.

"But seriously, Paige, Piper's right," Phoebe said, dropping her toast's crust back on the tray. "We heard some not-so-comforting stuff last night."

"Like what?" Paige asked, continuing to eat.

"Like their new plan is to scare you off so that Colin can't get married. Like the bad guys have infiltrated the castle before," Piper told her. "These people are not happy campers, Paige. And you're the evil camp director they want to run out of town."

"You're mixing metaphors there, sweetie," Paige said.

"That's what you're focusing on?" Piper asked. "Paige, these people are serious."

"Eh. It takes a lot to scare me," Paige said, waving a hand. "Besides, as you guys have witnessed firsthand, I am very well protected."

Piper glanced at Phoebe. Paige was acting a little blasé about this whole threat-to-her-safety thing. And was it just Piper, or was her sister talking like she was actually planning on sticking around this wacky palace? Piper's eyes instinctively traveled to Paige's left hand. Her stomach turned when she saw a fat diamond gleaming on her sister's ring finger.

"Paige, why are you wearing that ring?" Phoebe asked, noticing the rock at the same moment as Piper.

Paige lifted her hand and looked down at the

diamond as if she had forgotten it was there.

"Don't tell me you've decided to go through with this," Piper said, her mouth going dry as the words tumbled out.

Paige took a deep breath and let it out audibly. "Actually, I have," she said. "In fact, I'm meeting with the royal seamstress in about fifteen minutes to talk about a wedding gown."

Piper could hardly breathe. What had happened to her sister at this ball? Had there been some kind of brainwashing ritual? How could Leo have let this happen? And where the heck was he this morning, anyway?

Okay, let's focus on the disaster at hand here, she told herself.

"Paige—"

"Piper, I know you think this is crazy, but I've made my decision," Paige said, sitting forward. "I've been asked to do something monumentally important here. I've been asked to save thousands of innocents. Isn't that what we're supposed to do?"

"Well, yes, but—"

"I really want you guys to support me in this," Paige said firmly. "But even if you don't, I'm going to go through with it. You didn't see them last night, all grateful and hopeful and relieved. I want to help these people. I need to."

There was a long moment of silence during which Piper felt as if she was swallowing her own heart. Before she could put her hundreds of thoughts into coherent words, there was a knock on the door and Corinne walked in, followed by a trail of three servants.

"Good morning!" she said, looking pale but chipper. "I thought you might want some company for your meetings this morning. You should probably have someone with you who knows the customs and things."

"Thanks," Paige said.

"Lady Paige? Are you through?" a young girl asked, stepping up to the bed.

"Yes, thank you," Paige said. Phoebe grabbed another piece of toast as the girl cleared the tray away.

"Come on. Let's get you dressed," Corinne said, smiling at Paige and her sisters.

Paige swung her legs over the side of the bed and followed Corinne toward the dressing area where the servants waited. Piper felt utterly helpless. How was she supposed to talk her sister out of becoming princess of Tarsina when some of the people she was going to save were standing right there in the room?

"Paige? Don't you think we should talk a little bit more?" Piper suggested.

Paige paused and turned around very slowly. With the sunlight behind her and her chin held high, Piper couldn't help but notice that her sister already looked quite regal.

"There's nothing to talk about," Paige said flatly.

Then she joined her staff by the mirror to prepare for her first day as a royal bride-to-be. Piper and Phoebe looked at each other across the wide bed of tangled sheets and blankets.

"Think she's under a spell?" Phoebe asked.

"I wish, but no," Piper said, her heart heavy. "I think she's really determined to do this. And we all know that when Paige decides to do something . . ."

"It's pretty much done," Phoebe finished.

"This place is so beautiful," Paige said, taking a deep breath of the fresh, rose-scented air.

"Yeah. We like it," Colin replied with a smile.

Paige leaned back on her elbows in the lush grass. She was dressed in a gorgeous-but-binding red gown and had a feeling that a "lady" didn't normally sprawl out like this, but at that moment all she wanted to do was soak up as much sun as possible.

Corinne and her father, Richmond, set out the last of the dishes from the picnic basket and sat down on either side of Paige. Richmond had been Colin's tutor up until a couple of years ago, and it was through him that Corinne and Colin had met. Paige had been introduced to him as she, Colin, and Corinne had headed out to the gardens with their lunch. He was a handsome older man with salt-and-pepper hair and intelligent brown eyes. Paige had also discovered that he was very inquisitive.

"So, Paige, tell me, how are witches treated in your part of the world?" he asked, folding his legs up.

"We're not," Paige said, sitting up again. "No one really knows we exist."

"They have to hide," Corinne said, biting into an apple. "Pretend they're like everyone else."

Colin grabbed a napkin and wiped a stream of apple juice from Corinne's chin before it could stain her dress. They smiled at each other and he touched the napkin to her nose in a familiar gesture before he noticed Paige watching and busied himself opening containers of food.

"It's awful," Colin said. "She and her sisters can't even practice their magic in public."

"It sounds stifling, but sometimes it's better to hide who we truly are," Richmond said.

"Can't say I've ever heard that argument before," Paige told him.

"I know, it's not a common opinion," Richmond said with a small smile. "But I have often wished there was some way to cloak my true nature and that of my daughter. If we could somehow pass for magical people . . ."

"You could avoid the curse," Paige said slowly.

"Exactly," Richmond said, his eyes sad.

Paige could see the fear pass through all of them at the mention of the curse. These people were doomed, and they knew exactly when their deaths would come. Paige couldn't even imagine what it must be like to live that way.

"I just don't understand how she could do this to us," Corinne said, putting her fruit aside. "How could anyone do this to her people?"

"It's going to be okay now," Colin said. "Paige is here to help us."

Paige tried to smile, but her face was tight with anguish. Corinne didn't even look at her, anyway. It was like she suddenly couldn't, even though they had spent the entire morning laughing and talking together.

Colin reached over and squeezed Corinne's hand, then, finding that wasn't enough to comfort her, he moved toward her and folded her into his arms. Corinne pressed her face into his shirt and curled toward him. Paige felt the love between them and it made her heart break. These two had found each other, found their true loves, only to be torn apart in the most horrifying way possible.

Paige saw Colin whisper something in Corinne's ear and averted her gaze. How could she watch this? Watch the man she was supposed to marry in such an intimate moment with his true love? She glanced at Richmond and saw him watching the two lovers with tears in his eyes. This was almost too much for Paige to bear.

"I'm going to take Corinne for a walk around the pond," Colin said, standing. "You don't mind, Paige?"

"Of course not," Paige said, her voice thick.

Corinne pushed herself to her feet and let

Colin lead her away, his arm around her shoulders. Paige felt as if her heart had torn free from her chest. Richmond gazed at her, his expression unreadable.

"You must hate me," Paige said, looking down at the folds of her skirt.

"On the contrary," he replied. "You're my savior. You're my daughter's savior. Our people owe everything to you."

"I'm not a savior," she said with a scoff. "And all I'm doing right now is breaking your daughter's heart."

Richmond reached over and took Paige's hand in his. She looked into his eyes, and his gaze was steady and sure.

"Corinne knows that this is the only way," he said. "We all know it. We all accept it. And we are all grateful."

Paige smiled sadly and looked past the wise man to his daughter. She and Colin were standing on the far side of the glistening pond, staring into each other's eyes. Colin reached up and gently brushed a tear from Corinne's cheek, then pressed his lips to the spot where the tear had been. They held each other for a long moment that seemed to stretch out for hours.

Paige took a deep breath. She knew what she had to do.

"I don't understand, Leo," Piper railed, pacing the length of Paige's palace chamber. "Do you *want* Paige to leave us? Do you *want* to break up the Power of Three?"

"Piper, you know Leo doesn't want that," Phoebe said, attempting to calm her sister.

"Stay out of it, Phoebe," Piper said, her eyes flashing.

Phoebe snapped her mouth closed and sent Leo a helpless look. They both knew that when Piper got on a roll like this, there wasn't much they could do until she got it out of her system.

"You were supposed to watch over her while we were gone," Piper said, opening her hands in front of him. "This is what you *do.* This is your calling. When did you get so bad at it?"

"Piper, I did watch over her," Leo said in a soothing voice.

"Then why did you let him get her alone?" Piper demanded.

"What did you want me to do? Tackle the prince in front of his entire kingdom?" Leo asked.

"If you had to," Piper said, turning her profile to him.

"The truth is, it wouldn't have mattered what I did," Leo said, walking over to Piper. "We all know that Paige had to make up her own mind about this. And I think that on some level, you know she's made the right decision."

"No, I don't know that," Piper said, glancing at him for a split second.

Her words said one thing, but her voice said another. Phoebe knew that Piper was coming around to the realization that they were all having. Colin's birthday was mere days away. Time was running out and these people were counting on Paige to save them. It was a simple, age-old equation: Do or die. Die by the thousands.

"I still think we should talk to her," Piper said finally, letting out a sigh.

"We will, sweetie. As soon as she gets back," Phoebe said, joining them in a little circle near the foot of the bed. She checked her watch and her brow furrowed. "It's already after four. When was the last time a picnic lunch took five hours?"

Phoebe heard voices out in the hallway that sounded like Corinne's and Colin's. Her heart pounding with some unnamed concern, she jogged out of Paige's bedroom before the pair could disappear into one of the many winding passages of the castle.

"Prince Colin!" she called out, her voice echoing down the stone hall.

Shoes scratched against the silty stone floor, and a moment later Colin and Corinne appeared from around a corner. Their faces were flushed from being in the sun, and Corinne's hair had been blown free of its braid. They looked for all the world like a pair of lovers who had just returned from a date. Paige was not with them. Phoebe glanced up at the guards by the door

and hastened over to Colin. After the little meeting she and Piper had witnessed the night
before, Phoebe couldn't trust anyone inside the
castle.

"Is everything okay, Phoebe?" Colin asked,
glancing over her shoulder as Piper and Leo
joined them.

"Yeah, everything's fine," Phoebe said, looking behind her. The guards didn't seem to even
notice they were there. "We were just wondering
if you've seen Paige."

Colin's expression clouded. "She left us about
a half hour ago," he said, glancing at Corinne for
confirmation.

"She said she was going to find you guys,"
Corinne added, clearly concerned.

Phoebe's heart thumped extra hard, and she
turned around to face Piper and Leo. This was
not the kind of thing a girl wanted to hear when
there was an evil alliance out to "scare off" her
sister. "Where is she?"

Leo closed his eyes for a split second, and
then his face settled into a sort of resigned clar-
ity. "Come on. I know where she is," he said,
taking Phoebe's and Piper's hands. "Don't
worry," he told Colin. "We'll be back."

The three of them orbed out of the palace, and
seconds later Phoebe found herself standing in
the center of the attic back at the Manor. Paige
was standing near the window in a deep red
gown, flipping through the Book of Shadows

like the pages were on fire. The desperation in the room was palpable.

"Paige?" Phoebe said.

"Can't talk now. I'm working," Paige said without lifting her eyes.

"Are you home now?" Piper asked gently. "I mean, for good?"

"Not exactly," Paige said, sniffling. "I just . . . I have to find a way for Colin and Corinne to get married. I mean, there *has* to be a way. This whole magical discrimination thing is just wrong, and I can't believe that there's nothing in this stupid book to fix it."

She slammed the Book of Shadows closed and then glared at it as if it had betrayed her. Phoebe's heart went out to her sister. Clearly something had happened that afternoon that had tied her all up in knots.

"Paige, come here and sit down," Phoebe said, walking over to her sister and taking her hand. Paige's skin was hot to the touch and she felt limp—defeated. She tromped over to the couch and slumped down, her huge skirt fanning out over the floor. Phoebe and Piper sat down on either side of her while Leo stood before them, looking on with concern.

"What is it? What happened?" Piper asked.

"It's just . . . you should see them together," Paige said. "They're so in love. It isn't fair, Piper. They should be able to be together. I mean, this is the twenty-first century! What kind of person would curse her own ancestors like this?"

"She lived in a different time," Leo said. "I'm sure she was scared of change. She probably thought she was protecting her people, not harming them."

"Yeah, well, she has my vote for weakest witch of all time," Paige grumbled. She leaned her head back and stared at the ceiling. "There has to be something we can do."

"Paige, I hate to say this, but there's not," Phoebe told her. "Colin said it himself. They tried everything. He can't marry Corinne and still save Tarsina."

"But, Paige, that doesn't mean that you have to drop your whole life," Piper said gently. "You didn't put the curse on Tarsina, and you don't have to be the one to solve this problem. That's a lot of pressure to put on one person."

"I know," Paige said, lifting her head again. "But I said I would do it and I'm going to do it. And once I'm married I'm going to be the only woman in the world who's best friends with her husband's mistress," she added with a grim little smile.

Phoebe's heart felt like it was about to overflow. She was so proud of her sister's bravery. She was in awe of her willingness to sacrifice everything. But at the same time she was a little worried. What would become of the Charmed Ones once Paige was married and princess of another realm? Her sister was going to have a life on a whole other plane of existence. Would anything ever be the same again?

"What are you guys thinking?" Paige asked, looking from Phoebe to Piper.

Piper's eyes were full of tears, but she was smiling. "I was just thinking that you are one strong witch," she said.

"And I was just thinking about how proud I am of my little sister," Phoebe added.

"Thanks, guys," Paige said, a tear slipping down her cheek. "You have no idea how much that means to me."

Phoebe and Piper both grabbed Paige from either side and hugged her tight. Squeezing her eyes shut against the pain in her chest, Phoebe promised herself that she would be there for Paige over the next few days, no matter what. That's what sisters of future princesses were for.

Chapter Seven

The seamstress to the royal family had her very own studio on the top floor of the palace. One full wall of the room was made of floor-to-ceiling windows, allowing for the most amazing light of any room in the entire kingdom. Beautiful fabrics in a myriad of colors were draped over every available surface. Mannequins built in the exact measurements of the royal family members stood about the room in various stages of dress. In the very center of the chamber was a semicircle of at least ten huge mirrors around a small round stage.

Paige stood on this small stage wearing a gown that was beyond anything her overactive childhood imagination had ever conjured. She could see every detail from every angle and each glance took her breath away. So this was what it was like to be a princess.

"Oh, Paige. You were meant to wear that gown," Corinne said, holding her hand to her chest. She was standing behind Paige, but Paige could see her in several of the mirrors. Pain and regret filled Corinne's eyes as she looked Paige up and down and forced a smile.

Paige's heart went out to Corinne, and she turned to face her for real. The skirts swished around her as she moved, then settled like light little clouds around her feet.

"Are you sure you want to be here?" Paige asked softly. "I know if my man were marrying someone else, I would want to be as far away from the proceedings as possible."

"No, I think this is good for me," Corinne said, taking a deep breath and lifting her chin. "The more I'm here, the easier it'll be for me to accept that this is really happening, that I'm really going to have to give him up."

Corinne's voice cracked slightly on her last words, but she managed a smile.

Paige nodded, impressed with Corinne's bravery, but inside she felt sick to her stomach. If love could cause a person this much pain, maybe it wasn't all it was cracked up to be.

"Besides, if I weren't here I wouldn't get to be one of the first people to see this," Corinne said, lifting her hands in Paige's direction. "You look so beautiful."

"It's not me, it's this dress," Paige said, happy to change the subject. They all knew they were in an impossible situation. There was really no use in dwelling on the negatives.

Paige glanced at Marjorie, the wiry, gray-haired seamstress, who paced around her inspecting every seam, every bead, every fold. Her own dress was a plain, basic black with white lace around the collar. Pins stuck out of a pincushion that was fastened around her wrist by a thick red ribbon. Paige wasn't sure why she had them, though. She had been using her magic to make adjustments all afternoon. Not a single pin had been touched.

"This gown is incredible, Marjorie," Paige said. There was something sticking into her side from the bodice, but she tried to ignore it. The woman had done so much work already, and Paige didn't want to seem like a whining little princess.

"Not quite. Not yet," Marjorie said, pausing with her hand to her chin and narrowing her eyes. "It needs something . . ."

She waved her bony hand in the air and a dozen pale pink ribbons appeared in her grasp. A look of pure concentration settled on her face as she stared at the satin in her hand. This woman was intense. Paige caught Corinne's eyes in the mirror and they exchanged a private smile.

"Here," Marjorie said, opening her hand. The ribbons floated through the air as if dancing on the end of invisible strings. They swirled around Paige like she was a maypole, and she laughed as the soft fabric tickled her skin. Finally, under

Marjorie's watchful gaze, the ribbons settled around the skirt of the dress, running down at even intervals from the waistline and disappearing in the folds of the gown.

Paige checked the results and her eyes widened. She wouldn't have thought it possible, but the dress was even more perfect.

"A little color, that was what it was missing," Marjorie said, looking satisfied. "How do you like it, Lady Paige?"

"It's incredible," Paige repeated. She took a deep breath and winced. Okay, she couldn't ignore that little tightness at her side any longer. Not if she was supposed to meet and greet tens of thousands of Tarsinian citizens wearing this gown.

"There's just a little something sticking into me right here," she added, pointing to the edge of the bodice, right where it met the skirt. "Could get a little uncomfortable after a couple of hours."

"Here?" Marjorie asked, placing her hands on Paige's waist.

Paige nodded and Marjorie's eyebrows knit. There was a sudden wash of warmth around the dress's bodice and then the uncomfortable poking was gone.

"Wow. Nice," Paige said, taking a deep breath and sighing in relief. "What did you do?"

"Just shortened the boning," Marjorie said, slapping her hands together. "No problem."

There was a swift knock on the large doors to the studio and they swung open with a loud creak. A tall gentleman with a purposeful expression strode in and dropped into a low bow before Paige.

"Pardon the interruption, Lady Paige . . . ladies," he said, nodding to Corinne and Marjorie. "I am Paulo Partina, the royal florist. I've come with some samples for the wedding ceremony and was hoping you would be so kind as to look them over."

"Uh . . . sure," Paige said with a shrug.

Her eyes widened as a troop of workers walked in, each carrying a huge flower arrangement that was more exquisite than the last. The entire room filled with a thick, intoxicating cocktail of scents that seemed to overwhelm Paige's senses.

"Wow, Paulo," Corinne said, her eyes widening. "You've really outdone yourself this time."

"Well, it is not every day that the crown prince of our realm is wed," Paulo said with a smile. "Now, Lady Paige, which color scheme do you prefer?" he asked.

Paige looked over the arrangements, which were held out for her inspection. The first was made up of pink and white roses, a classic choice. The second was overflowing with purple hydrangeas, hot pink flowers, and lavender accents. The third was completely white, comprised of all sorts of lilies. The last was like a starburst of oranges and reds made up of mums and daisies and wildflowers.

"They're all amazing," Paige said, reaching out to touch the soft petals on one of the roses. Suddenly, faced with all these choices, she felt as if everything was happening so fast. Last week her biggest decision had been whether to have a turkey panini or a Cobb salad for lunch. Now she was picking out flowers for her *wedding*.

Paige swallowed hard and took a step back, her mind swimming. The smells overwhelmed her and she felt herself start to swoon. Suddenly, thanks to Marjorie, a large chair flew over from the other side of the room and Paige sat back into it.

"Are you all right?" Corinne asked, coming to Paige's side.

"I'm fine," Paige said. "It's just . . . a lot to take in." She drew a long breath and attempted to calm her confused heart. "What do you think, Corinne? Which would you choose?"

"Oh . . . it's . . . it's your wedding, Paige. Not mine," Corinne said.

"I know, but I want you to pick," Paige replied. "Come on, you'll go down in history as the woman who chose the color scheme for the wedding of the century."

Corinne bit her lip and glanced up at Paulo. "The wildflowers," she said without hesitation. "They're Colin's favorite. He loves the fields outside the palace grounds. He loves the free-dom they represent."

Paulo nodded, but still looked to Paige for confirmation. For a second this took Paige aback. She wasn't used to being the final word on anything. But she supposed she was going to have to become accustomed to the feeling. Still, she didn't like the way Corinne was being disrespected.

"You heard her. Wildflowers," Paige said. "Thank you, Paulo."

"Thank you, Lady Paige," he said, dropping another low bow.

He clapped his hands and his workers marched out. Paulo followed them and closed the door. Instantly the pink ribbons Marjorie had added to the dress lifted away and were replaced by light yellow ones. Paige shot Marjorie a questioning look.

"To match the flowers," she said with a kind smile.

"Thanks," Paige said faintly. These people were nothing if not on the ball.

"You sure you're okay?" Corinne asked Paige, crouching at her feet.

"I'm sure," Paige said, her heart full as she looked down at the girl who should have been wearing her gown, who should have had servants bowing to her, who, by all rights, was the true princess. "I'm just really glad you're here."

Phoebe grasped the heavy door handle on the front door of St. John's Pub and pulled. The thick smell of stale beer and smoke wafted out of the bar, polluting the street.

"Nice place," Leo said under his breath.

"You were expecting the bad guys to hang out in a day spa, maybe?" Piper said wryly.

Phoebe smiled and rolled her eyes. All was not well in Piper-and-Leo Land just yet. She just hoped they wouldn't squabble in front of Sinjin. Phoebe hadn't even met the guy yet, but she had a feeling he wouldn't be the type of person who would appreciate having his time wasted by couples' banter.

"Put your game faces on, kids," Phoebe told them. "We're goin' in."

She stepped into the pub. The tables weren't nearly as packed as they had been the night before, but there were still a few wretches and drunks milling about. Holding her head high, Phoebe met the gaze of anyone who dared look her way. She had learned long ago that the only way to gain respect was to act like she owned any room she walked into. Even the dens of evil.

Phoebe, Piper, and Leo stepped up to the nearly deserted bar and Leo cleared his throat. The barmaid from the night before stopped cleaning the glasses and looked up. Her already surly expression darkened when she saw her customers.

"You again," she said, sneering.

"We said we'd be back," Piper replied coolly.

"We want to see Sinjin," Phoebe put in.

"You do, do you?" the woman asked, placing a smudged bar glass down in front of her. She pressed her beefy hands into the surface of the bar and leaned forward, giving Phoebe an unnecessary view of her ample cleavage. "And what makes you think he'll want to see you?"

"We have something he wants," Leo said. "Information he might find very interesting."

Nice one, Phoebe thought. *Keep it vague.*

The barmaid's beady eyes slid over Leo's face and down over his solid frame. She didn't seem impressed, but she also didn't wave him off.

"They're meeting in the back," she said, tilting her head in that direction. "But they don't let just anyone in. You're gonna hafta prove you belong there."

What the heck does that mean? Phoebe thought, but of course didn't say. The last thing she wanted was to look confused or thrown. Instead she kept her expression blank and led Piper and Leo through the bar to a darkened hallway in the back. She paused at the end of the corridor when she saw the size of the guard waiting at the other end. He was twice Leo's girth and had at least six inches on him. He wore black leather pants and a black tunic. The moment he noticed his visitors he took a step forward, away from the door he was guarding.

"What's your business here?" he said, his voice scratchy, like he had just come from screaming all night at a rock concert.

"We're here for the meeting," Phoebe replied. "We want to talk to Sinjin."

"Demonstrate your powers," the guard said without batting an eyelash. "Only people of pure magic can enter."

Phoebe glanced back at Piper, and she nodded ever so slightly. Phoebe levitated off the ground about three feet and hovered there. The guard nodded. Piper lifted her hands and blew up a nearby chair, shattering it to bits. The man nodded again. Then Leo disappeared in a swirl of white light. For the first time, the guard looked around and registered surprise. Then Leo appeared behind him and tapped him on the shoulder. The guard whirled around, saw Leo, and smiled.

"Nice work," he said.

"Thanks," Leo replied with a modest shrug.

The guard reached past him and turned to unlatch the door, stepping aside to let them pass. Murmured voices spilled out into the hall, peppered with a smattering of applause. With one last look over her shoulder, Phoebe slipped past the guard and walked into the meeting.

Part of her was expecting a cinematic moment in which the entire room would fall silent at their entrance and all eyes would turn to inspect the new visitors. Luckily, there was no such response. The room was filled with people, sitting at tables, standing along the walls, lounging in a gallery up above, but no one even noticed Phoebe, Piper, and

Leo as they stepped inside and found a spot near the back. All eyes were riveted on the speaker, who paced the front of the room.

Tall and broad with blond hair and angular features, the man who had caught everyone's attention had an intense, almost maniacal look in his dark eyes. Beads of perspiration clung to his forehead as he paced, railing on about the impure blood that poisoned the kingdom of Tarsina. Every now and then, one of his comments was met with a raucous round of applause. There was a certain power about him, a certain charisma, that made him seriously sexy.

Too bad he's also a psycho, Phoebe thought, following his every move with her eyes. Every word out of his mouth was either bigoted or crass or obviously intended to incite the crowd.

"Sinjin?" Piper said under her breath.

"I'm thinking yeah," Phoebe replied.

"And now, this new lady . . . this *Charmed One* has come in to save us all," Sinjin said sarcastically, glaring at the crowd. "Does she not know what she is saving? I would think that a member of the most revered magical family on earth would see that what we are trying to do here is for the Greater Good!"

This comment was met with a huge, angry cheer, and Phoebe's heart twisted into a million knots. How could anyone think that she and her sisters would want thousands of people to die? If these pure magical Tarsinians knew anything about them, they should know that they were dedicated to saving all Innocents, without prejudice. It made her sick to think that these people were willing to see half their population keel over and die.

"This Paige has put a kink in our plans," Sinjin continued. "If she and the prince do marry tomorrow, Tarsina will go on to exist as it is. And every day we will continue to be corrupted until our way of life deteriorates into nothing. Into the very dust under your feet."

A few people actually looked blankly down at their shoes.

"Do we want that to happen?"

"NO!" everyone in the room shouted, raising their fists in the air.

"We have to do something!" the skinny man who had been in the bar the night before cried out, standing up from a chair near the front of the room. "We have to shake this Paige girl up. We must find a way to frighten her away."

His words were met with a slightly less emphatic cheer, and Sinjin held up his hands to quiet the people.

"It's too late for innocuous little plans," he said. "We tried to manipulate the situation through subtle means and it didn't work. Sending that mortal girl in to steal the prince's heart seemed clever at the time, but we should have known that Prince Colin would rank the needs of his people over the needs of his heart."

All the air rushed out of Phoebe's lungs. *Sending that mortal girl in . . .*

Someone spat on the floor at Phoebe's feet, but she barely noticed. Her mind was too busy reeling. She looked at Piper and Leo and knew that they had heard it too—that she wasn't just imagining things.

"Corinne?" Phoebe whispered hoarsely. "Corinne is a bad guy?"

"But she will serve her purpose now," Sinjin continued with a sinister smile.

"But how?" the skinny man asked, his eyes wide. "Colin has already announced his betrothal to Lady Paige."

"Oh, she has a new purpose," Sinjin said. "I sent her a message this morning. If she values her life . . . and the life of her father . . . she'll do as I ask."

"What did you ask?" someone in the gallery shouted.

Sinjin took a long drink from a black beer stein and licked his lips slowly before turning his eyes to the gallery. "I asked her . . . to kill the witch."

Phoebe gasped audibly, but no one heard her. They were too busy shouting and cheering and dancing and laughing. Celebrating the idea of murdering her own sister. Before·Phoebe could even realize what she was doing, she had stepped away from Piper and Leo. Piper tried to grasp her hand, but Phoebe batted her sister away. She couldn't let this happen. She couldn't stand here and stay quiet while hundreds of people rallied around the upcoming death of her little sister.

"No!" Phoebe shouted as loudly as she could. "No! No! No!"

Gradually the people around Phoebe started to quiet. They turned toward her with confused and appalled expressions. Up at the front of the room, Sinjin grabbed a chair and stepped up onto it to better see the person who was contradicting him. His eyes narrowed when he saw Phoebe.

"Who are you?" he asked.

Phoebe swallowed hard. She couldn't exactly give them her name. They all knew of the Charmed Ones.

"I am loyal to the cause, sir," she said, bile rising up in her throat as she bowed to the evil bastard.

"Are you?" he asked, stepping down again. The crowd parted to allow Sinjin to approach Phoebe. "Then why, might I ask, are you questioning my plan?"

An excited little murmur passed through the crowd, and Phoebe knew they were all salivating to see what Sinjin might do to her.

"I'm not questioning you," Phoebe replied, standing up straight and looking him in the eye. She tried not to shudder in the face of the malice that was pouring off him. "I just don't trust this Corinne girl."

She glanced over her shoulder at Piper and Leo, silently requesting some backup. Leo stepped away from the wall, while Piper remained hidden among the crowd. It was quick thinking on her part, since three new witches might arouse some suspicion—even in a magical kingdom.

"She's right," Leo said, standing tall. "The girl didn't succeed on her first assignment. What reason do we have to believe that she'll carry this one through?"

"She will. If she wants to live," Sinjin said, dismissing them as he turned away.

We have to do something, Phoebe thought, racking her brain. Right then all she could think about was getting back to Paige. They had to protect her. They had to find Corinne.

"We should send someone to the castle, then, to make sure everything goes smoothly," Phoebe suggested. "Someone to make sure the girl actually does as you've asked."

"And how do you suggest we get inside?" Sinjin asked, facing them again.

"My brother is a member of the prince's guard," Phoebe said, grasping Leo's arm. "He can come and go as he pleases. He can get us in."

"Really?" Sinjin asked, his eyes sliding over Leo. "You work for the prince, yet you are loyal to the cause?"

"The prince doesn't know his own mind," Leo said flatly. "He doesn't realize what he's doing to the kingdom."

Sinjin's eyes narrowed to near-slits as he studied Phoebe and Leo and considered their plan. Finally he nodded, ever so slowly.

"Fine. You two will go to the castle and report back when the deed is done," Sinjin said, slapping a hand down on Leo's shoulder. "Lord knows the royal family won't let us know of Lady Paige's death. The mortals would be panicking in the streets," he said with a laugh.

His followers echoed his mirth.

"Go!" Sinjin ordered Phoebe and Leo. "I expect to see you here this evening. And with good news."

Phoebe and Leo gave a quick bow and headed for the door, followed soon after by Piper.

"Orb us back, Leo," Piper said, grasping his arm as soon as they were out of earshot of the guard. "We have to get to Paige before Corinne does."

Leo nodded and orbed them out of the pub. Phoebe had only one thought before swirling off in a whirlwind of white light.

I just hope we're not too late. . . .

Chapter Eight

"Paige!" Piper shouted, the second she appeared in the center of Paige's bedroom at the castle. Her pulse was racing a mile a minute and her adrenaline was so high she could have blown up the whole place with one swing of her hands. "Paige! Where are you?"

She, Phoebe, and Leo fanned out, checking every corner of the massive chamber. Phoebe dove into the walk-in closet and tore through the packed racks of clothing while Piper checked the bathroom and Leo headed into the attached sitting room. Suddenly the doors behind them swung open and the guard stepped in from the hallway.

"How did you get in here?" he asked.

"Forget that. Where's my sister?" Piper demanded.

"All I know is she isn't here," he said, glancing across the room as Phoebe emerged from the closet. "So you can stop tearing her quarters apart."

"You have no idea where she went?" Leo asked.

"No. I'm sorry, sir. If I were you I would ask the prince," the guard said, squaring his shoulders. "They are engaged to be married, after all. If anyone would know where Lady Paige is, Prince Colin would."

Piper narrowed her eyes at the guard, somehow restraining herself from choking him. *She* was the one who should know where her sister was. Not some random guy who just walked into their lives less than two weeks ago. This situation had long since gotten out of hand.

"Fine," she said, tossing her hair back. "We'll ask the prince. Come on, Phoebe."

Piper led Phoebe and Leo out into the hallway and stalked down to the royal chamber where the king, the queen, and Colin seemed to spend most of their time. The guards parted to let them pass, and Piper stalked into the sundrenched room. Courtiers lounged about, laughing, talking, working on needlepoint, and listening to the musicians, who were playing a peppy little tune. A few maids folded tapestries into baskets in the corner. The royal family was gathered in a little clump by their thrones, their heads bent close together as they talked in hushed voices.

Suddenly Piper saw red. This whole thing

was Colin's family's fault—theirs and their stupid, sadistic, prejudiced ancestor's. Look at them, standing there as if everything was fine. As if their kingdom wasn't one huge, massively dysfunctional family. As if they hadn't dragged an innocent witch into the mayhem to save their skins. At that moment, fearing for Paige's life, Piper could have killed them. Why couldn't these people clean up their own messes and leave her family out of it?

"Colin! Where's Paige?" Piper shouted, storming across the room.

Colin stood up and looked at them, confused.

"You do not address the prince of Tarsina in that manner," the queen snapped, her eyes flashing.

They all ignored her, including Colin, who clearly sensed something was wrong. "She's out riding. With Corinne."

Piper felt as if someone had just yanked the stone floor out from beneath her feet. *This isn't happening*, she thought wildly. *This just can't be happening*.

"Where?" Phoebe asked. "Where would she have taken her?"

"She didn't *take* her anywhere," Colin said defensively, picking up on Phoebe's accusatory tone. "They went together."

"What's this all about?" the king asked, standing behind his son.

"This is about my sister's life being in danger,"

Piper said, glaring at Colin. "And your little girl-friend's the one who's been assigned to kill her."

The queen paled, and Colin's face went slack. "Corinne? No. That's not possible. She would never hurt anyone."

Leo took a few steps away from the group and closed his eyes, concentrating. Piper had never been so happy that her husband had that special tracking power. It was about the only thing that could help them right then.

"Yeah, well, you better hope you're right," Piper said.

"I've got her," Leo said from behind Piper. "I know where she is. Let's go."

Piper cast one last glare over her shoulder at the royal family and grabbed her husband's hand.

"If anything happens to my sister, you're not going to want to be here when I get back," she said. Then, in a flash, she was gone.

"Thank you for bringing me out here," Paige said, taking a long, deep breath of fresh air. The castle was so far off in the distance it looked more like a cottage with a lot of windows. The farther Paige rode, the more at peace she felt. "I really needed a break from all the crazy wedding planning."

"It's no problem," Corinne said with a smile. "I haven't been this far out from the castle in weeks."

"Really?" Paige asked, holding the reins a bit

bit tighter as her horse clomped through a shallow stream. "Why not?"

"Well, I used to ride out here all the time. Riding is like my way of meditating, you know? Of getting away from it all," Corinne said, leaning forward to stroke her horse's mane. "But for the past few weeks all Colin and I have been doing is working on a solution to the curse. I didn't really have time to take long rides."

"And now you've found me," Paige said, then flushed. "The solution."

"Yes. I suppose so," Corinne said quietly, averting her gaze.

"Corinne, I want you to know that whatever happens, I'm not going to stop you from seeing Colin," Paige said as a breeze lifted her hair from her face. "You know that, right?"

Corinne smiled slightly. "I know," she said. "It's still reassuring to hear it, though."

Paige returned her smile and looked out at the trail ahead. The slim dirt path they were following wound its way through a grassy field, then disappeared into a thick wood. Paige wondered how far Corinne was planning on taking her, but said nothing. She was enjoying herself. For the first time since she had arrived in Tarsina, she felt seminormal.

"Can you believe you're getting married tomorrow?" Corinne asked.

A weightless and not entirely pleasant sensation took over Paige's body and she gripped the reins again, trying to ground herself. This was not the way she wanted to feel on the day before her wedding—so scared and uncertain. But she knew she was doing the right thing, as much as it differed from everything she had ever dreamed of.

"No. Not really," she said. "But let's not talk about that right now. Tell me something about you and Colin." For some reason, Paige was salivating to hear a romantic story.

"Like what?" Corinne asked.

"Like . . . tell me how you met," Paige prompted.

A private little smile of pleasure lit Corinne's face and she stared down at her hands. "My father had been Colin's tutor for many years, but I had never been to the castle," Corinne said. "The queen wasn't happy that my father was teaching her son, so he never brought me to work. He feared she would use any excuse to fire him."

"Why wasn't she happy with your dad?" Paige asked, her brow knitting. "He seems like he would make an incredible teacher."

"Oh he is," Corinne said. "He's very wise and patient and kind. He's one of Tarsina's leading scholars. But he's of nonmagic blood."

Paige's heart skipped a foreboding beat. "The queen actually cares about that stuff?"

"I can't blame her," Corinne said with a shrug. "There are a lot of people in the kingdom who believe the old ways are the best ways. Even those who don't want the curse to come to pass . . . some of them educate their children only in the history of Tarsina and try not to let the outside world touch them. I suppose it's hard for them to let go."

"Yeah, but still, the woman is one of the leaders of the realm," Paige said. "It would be nice if she were a little more open-minded."

"True. But I believe she was just doing what she thought was best," Corinne replied.

"So, if that's the way she felt . . . how did your dad get the job?" Paige asked.

"Colin and his father wanted to hire him, and I think eventually the king put his foot down," Corinne said with a laugh. "He doesn't overrule her often. He saves it for the big decisions."

"Wow," Paige said as they came to the edge of the woods. "So, what does all this have to do with you and Colin?"

"Well, one day my father came home and said that they needed a new maid at the castle," Corinne explained, the shadows from the trees darkening her face. "He said that his superiors suggested that I might like the job. So I came to the palace with him the next day and was given one of the prime positions. I was put in charge of Colin's wardrobe."

"Oh, I see," Paige said with a smirk. "You bring him his clothes every morning and night and the sparks start to fly."

"Basically," Corinne said. "Colin had never

been very particular about his appearance, so I knew he liked me when he started wanting to change his clothes five and six times a day."

Paige and Corinne both laughed.

"It's so funny, isn't it?" Paige said. "You're kept away from the castle all that time and then, just like that, you're there and you and Colin fall in love. It's like fate brought you together."

The laughter faded from Corinne's face and she looked straight ahead at the path. They were moving deeper into the woods now and the trees were getting thick. The branches and leaves above nearly blocked out the sun. There was almost no sound other than the occasional rustling of leaves in the breeze. Paige wasn't the skittish type, but if she were this place would definitely have spooked her.

"Maybe we should head back," Paige suggested as her horse slowed its own steps. "My sisters are probably wondering where I am."

"Paige . . . there's something I need to tell you," Corinne said, pulling her horse up to a stop.

Paige did the same. She thought she heard, far off in the distance, the sound of racing hooves. Suddenly, for no apparent reason, her heart started to pound.

"What is it?" she asked, concerned at Corinne's sudden seriousness. "Is everything okay?"

"No," Corinne said, lifting her face. Tears swam in her light eyes. Her face was marked with angry red blotches. "No, everything's not okay."

Now Paige was certain of what she was hearing. A number of horses were heading their way at breakneck speed. Corinne reached into her saddlebag. Paige held her breath. What was going on here?

"Paige, I'm so . . . so . . . sorry—"

Suddenly Leo, Piper, and Phoebe orbed in right between the horses. Paige's mount whinnied and kicked up his front legs in surprise. Paige gripped the saddle's horn to steady herself as she fought to catch her breath.

"Paige! Get out of here!" Piper shouted.

"What? What's going on?" Paige asked, yanking on the reins to get her horse under control. He sidestepped away from Corinne into the trees at the far side of the path.

"It's Corinne! She's trying to kill you!" Phoebe said.

"What?" Corinne shouted, over the now deafening sound of approaching horses. "No! I would never—"

At that moment a dozen armored guards on huge, panting steeds raced into the tiny clearing. They surrounded Corinne and drew their swords, sending a metallic ringing through the trees and scaring a few birds into flight. Corinne's face lost all its color and for a moment, Paige was sure her new friend was going to faint.

"Corinne Van Den Pelt! You are under arrest

for the crime of conspiring against the royal family!" the rider at the front of the pack shouted.

Corinne opened her mouth to speak, but let out only a pathetic-sounding whimper. Paige moved her horse back up onto the trail and jumped down from the saddle.

"She didn't do anything!" Paige shouted up at the guards. "She would never hurt Colin and his family."

"Take her into custody," the man ordered one of his lackeys, completely ignoring Paige.

"No! Release her!" Paige shouted as a couple of men dragged Corinne down from her horse and bound her arms behind her. "I demand that you release her!"

Paige wasn't sure if she could get away with demanding anything, but she could think of nothing else to do. These men couldn't treat Corinne this way. She had sacrificed everything to help Colin save their people. She had even given up on true love.

"You don't have any authority here, Lady Paige," the man told her flatly, his gray eyes as hard as granite. "Not yet."

"Piper! Do something!" Paige said as Corinne was loaded onto the back of a guard's horse. Tears streamed down her face as she turned away from Paige. "Leo!"

"Paige, I'm sorry, honey, but it's true," Phoebe said gently. "Corinne is a loyalist. She was plotting to kill you."

Paige's heart sank into her toes. "No. It's not true," she said slowly. "She's my friend. Colin trusts her."

"We heard the plan with our own ears, Paige," Piper said, wrapping her arms around Paige. "She's not who you think she is."

Paige looked at the ground, the packed dirt of the trail swimming through her vision. She couldn't believe this was happening. She couldn't believe that five minutes ago everything was fine and now nothing she had believed was true.

The guards turned their horses around one by one and raced off toward the castle again, bringing their prisoner with them. With a heavy heart, Paige lifted her face and watched them go, her eyes full of confused, angry, unshed tears. Corinne had helped her so much over the past couple of days. They had planned together, laughed together, shared so many things. Paige couldn't believe that Corinne was anything but her friend. Her sisters had to be wrong this time. They just had to be.

Paige pressed her fingers into the cold stone wall of the dungeon as she trod carefully down the slim, winding steps. Lit only by the occasional torch attached to the wall, the stairs were slick and treacherous and seemed to go on forever, twisting down into the depths of the earth. Behind her was Luka, the guard who usually stood in front of her door. Colin had insisted she take Luka along with her to the dungeon for protection, and at first Paige had resisted. She still couldn't believe Corinne wanted to harm her, and she couldn't see how the girl could do anything if she was locked up in prison. But now she was glad that Luka had come along. This was a long trek to make without any company.

"We're almost there," Luka said, as if sensing her trepidation.

"I guess there aren't many successful escapes from this place," Paige said over her shoulder. The second she stopped concentrating, her foot slipped off the edge of a step and she almost went down. Luka grabbed her arm at the last second and steadied her.

"There's never been one," he said with a small smile.

Paige nodded her thanks and kept moving. It looked like Corinne was pretty much here to stay.

Finally, Paige came to a dirt floor at the bottom of the stairs. She had expected to see a line of barred cells, but instead she found herself in a vast open room with prisoners tethered to the walls by iron chains. This was a real, medieval-style dungeon. There wasn't a comfort in sight and the air was thick with the stench of sweat, human waste, and rotting food. It was all Paige could do to keep from retching.

"State your business," a tall man in a black

cloak demanded, stepping toward them. His pale skin was so taut Paige could make out the outlines of his skull. He looked more like a medieval executioner than a jailer.

"We're here to see Corinne," Paige said, ignoring her fluttering heart as she so often had to do in her line of business.

"Paige!"

Squinting through the darkness, Paige caught a glimpse of Corinne's white dress, now tattered and muddied. She stepped past executioner man, but he grabbed her arm and spun her around. Instantly, Luka had a vise grip on the jailer's neck.

"That's the Lady Paige, your future princess," Luka said. "I suggest you remove your hands."

Immediately, and with an awed expression, the jailer released Paige's arm.

"I'm sorry, miss," he said with a quick bow. "Forgive me."

Paige smiled at Luka. Apparently this guy was good to have around.

"Are you all right?" Paige asked, racing to Corinne's side.

"I'm fine," Corinne said. "I just stumbled a little coming down the stairs, that's all. Paige . . . what are you doing here? I thought you would never want to see me again."

"Are you kidding? I'm just sorry I didn't stop them back in the woods," Paige said. "I can't believe they think you have anything to do with the loyalists. I told them there was some kind of mistake—"

"There's no mistake, Paige," Corinne said quietly.

Paige's heart nearly stopped beating. "What?"

"It's all true," Corinne said, a single tear slipping down her cheek. "All the charges are true."

Paige's mind struggled to wrap itself around what she was hearing, but it couldn't. This just didn't make sense. Paige knew that Corinne loved Colin. She had seen them together. A person just couldn't fake emotion like that.

"I don't understand," Paige said.

"The loyalists . . . they blackmailed me into seducing Colin," Corinne said, tipping her head back against the jagged wall as the tears started to flow in earnest. "They're the ones who got me the job at the castle. They told me that I was to make Colin fall for me to prevent him from marrying a woman with pure blood."

"But that doesn't make any sense," Paige said. "If the curse comes true, you're one of the people who's going to die."

"No. They can protect me," Corinne said. "Me and my father. They promised to protect us from the curse."

"So that was the bribe," Paige said. "You get everyone else killed, but you'll be spared."

"I didn't want to do it, but they threatened to kill my entire family. My parents, my grandmother, my cousins and aunts and uncles. All of them," Corinne said. "I didn't know what else to do. I love them so much. I would do anything to protect them. But I never expected . . . I never expected that Colin and I would actually fall in love. And I do love him, Paige. I love him more than anything else in the world."

Paige stared at Corinne. Part of her knew she should hate this girl for everything she had done, but instead she just felt sorry for her. She was obviously tearing herself up inside. Paige knew what it felt like to be conflicted between duty and desire. She could only imagine the kind of pressure Corinne had been under during her days with Colin.

"I didn't mean for any of this to happen," Corinne whimpered. "Everything is just so out of control. And now . . . now there's nothing I can do. I can't help anyone from this dungeon."

Paige knew that all she had to do was orb Corinne out of there and the girl would be free again, but she also knew that her friend would have nowhere to go. The royal guard would only hunt her down again. Plus, if she helped Corinne escape, Paige would be under suspicion as well. Paige had never felt this helpless.

"There's something else," Corinne whispered. "I wanted to tell you in the woods this morning—"

"That's right. You were going to tell me something when the guards swooped in," Paige said.

Corinne nodded. "You have to be careful,

Paige. Last night I received a message from Sinjin, the leader of the loyalist movement. He ordered me to kill you."

Paige's stomach felt suddenly hollow. She had felt such fear back in the woods that morning, and she knew now that this was why. She had sensed that Corinne was a threat to her. At the time, she just hadn't been able to accept it.

"They'll hear about my arrest soon if they haven't already," Corinne said, her voice turning hoarse and desperate. "Paige, I'm sure they'll send someone else to do it. They're determined that the curse will come true."

Paige instinctively took a couple of steps back from Corinne. Her heel caught in a crack between two stones and she stumbled. Luka was there in a flash to steady her.

"Don't trust anyone," Corinne continued shrilly. "Believe me, these people will do anything to make sure the curse is fulfilled. Please, Paige. Please. Just be careful. All our lives depend on you."

Chapter Nine

"This can't be happening," Colin said. "It just can't be."

Paige was perched on the edge of the divan in her chamber, and she looked up at him with sympathetic eyes. For the past half hour all Colin had done was pace the room and repeat this same refrain. Every now and then he would stop, as if something had just occurred to him, and cover his face with his hands. Paige knew he felt as though his heart was being slowly torn from his chest. She knew he was grieving as deeply as if Corinne had been found dead. Maybe even more so. He had been betrayed by the person he loved most in the world. In some ways, it was even worse than if Corinne had died.

"Colin, I know this is difficult to hear, but I truly believe that Corinne really does love you,"

Paige said firmly. "Whatever her reasons for first coming to the castle, she fell in love with you once she was here."

Colin crossed his arms over his chest and scoffed, but Paige could see in his eyes that he wanted to believe this was true. He needed something to hold on to.

"How could she do this to us? To all of us?" Colin asked. "Why didn't she just tell us that she had been sent here by the loyalists? Didn't she know that we would have protected her?"

"Well, when she first came here she didn't know you that well," Paige reasoned. "She didn't know how you would react."

"And once she got to know me?" Colin asked, sitting down next to Paige. He laced his fingertips together and gripped his hands into a ball. "What then? Why didn't she tell me then?"

"I'm sure she was afraid of losing you," Paige said, gently placing her hand on Colin's back. "She had betrayed you. She must have been petrified of losing your trust."

"And for good reason," Colin muttered.

He pressed his lips together and looked down at the floor, his shoulders hunched. Paige had never seen him look so vulnerable. From the second they had met, Colin had been nothing but self-assured, confident, in charge. Now he looked like a lost little child.

"All she wants to do now is help," Paige told

him. "I really believe that. Maybe you should have her released. Show her that mercy. We can all figure this out together."

"I can't," Colin said. "I can't even imagine seeing her right now."

"She made a mistake, Colin, but she's still the girl you love," Paige said. "She wants you to marry me. She wants you to save the kingdom. She's willing to give up her future so that you can be the hero and your people can live."

Colin covered his mouth and nose with both hands and stared straight ahead. "I don't know."

"At least go and see her. Talk to her," Paige said. "Let her try to explain."

Colin looked at Paige and she could tell that he was considering it. That he badly wanted to believe that Corinne was still the woman he knew, that everything could be worked out. He started to speak, but not two words were out when the door to Paige's room swung open and Luka's voice boomed out.

"Her Majesty! The queen!"

Paige and Colin jumped to their feet as the queen swept into the room, the train of her emerald green dress swirling behind her. Her hair was pulled up in a tight braided bun and her skin was powdered white. She looked like a royal ghost come back to haunt the castle.

Paige dropped into a quick curtsy and the queen nodded at her to stand.

"Lady Paige, I've come to apologize for the incident this morning," the queen said, her voice clipped. "Believe me when I tell you that this Corinne will be severely punished."

"That's not necessary, Your Majesty," Paige said.

"It's nice to know you're a merciful woman, but perhaps we should leave such matters to those of us with experience," the queen said, looking down her long nose at Paige. "We can't abide a rebellion nor an assassination attempt, I'm sure you'll agree. At any rate, I want to make sure you are safe until the wedding, so the king and I have decided to triple the number of guards at your door."

"Mother, do you really think that's needed?" Colin asked.

"Colin, this woman is not only your bride-to-be, but she's to be the savior of Tarsina itself," the queen snapped. "So, yes, I do think it is needed."

"Maybe I should go talk to Corinne," Colin suggested to his mother. "Perhaps she can tell us something more. Give us some hint as to what we might expect."

The queen's eyes narrowed as Colin spoke, and she raised an authoritative hand to halt him. "I don't think that would be wise," she said. "I don't want you seeing that girl again, Colin, even in the dungeon. At least not until after you are married. She may be a mortal, but clearly she has powerful friends in magical circles. Evil magical circles. Who knows what they might be capable of?"

"But, Your Majesty," Paige interjected, "she's the only one who might have some information that could help us stop the loyalists."

"She's also the only one who has been able to infiltrate the castle, steal the prince's heart, and make an attempt on your life, my dear," the queen said. "Why give her the chance to talk to my besotted son and wheedle her way out of prison? No. I say we wait."

Paige wanted to point out that Corinne had made no move to hurt Paige and that when her saddlebag was checked, all that was found there were carrots for the horse and a half-dozen hand-kerchiefs—not exactly lethal weapons. If Corinne had been reaching for anything when the guards had come upon them in the woods, it had been a cloth to dry her eyes. But Paige knew better than to argue with a woman like the queen. Her Majesty had made up her mind. The only thing Paige could hope for now was a way to get around her.

"Fine, Mother. If that's what you think is best," Colin said finally, dejectedly.

"I'm glad you agree," she said with a tight smile. Then she turned to Paige. "You are not to leave this room unless you are accompanied by Luka and at least three of his men, is that under-stood?"

"Sure," Paige replied flatly, thinking, *I'll just orb out if I want to.*

"Good. I will see you both at dinner," the queen said. Then she turned and quickly left the room.

"I'm sorry about all this," Colin said, turning to Paige. "I know this isn't what you expected, but it's only until tomorrow afternoon. Then we'll be married and this nightmare will be over."

Paige swallowed hard, letting the words "we'll be married" sink slowly in. Between the potential assassins lurking outside the castle and her unbending future mother-in-law, Paige was really starting to wonder what her married life was going to be like.

"Yeah, until we have a kid and he or she is put through the same thing in twenty-five years," Paige muttered.

Colin smiled sadly. "It's a difficult cross to bear, but it's my duty," he said. "You'll come to understand it in time."

Paige didn't really think that she would, but she kept her mouth shut. She was tired of talking about curses and plots and duty. All she wanted was for things to work out the way they should. Unfortunately, that didn't look like it was about to happen any time soon.

"I have to go," Colin said. "I promised my father I would sit in on his security meeting. We're going over the plans for the wedding."

"Okay," Paige said, feeling suddenly exhausted. "I think I might take a nap anyway."

"I'll see you soon," Colin said, leaning forward and giving her a soft kiss on the cheek. "And, Paige, if I haven't said it before or enough, thank you."

Paige smiled slightly and nodded. As soon as Colin was gone, the heavy doors were closed behind him and Paige heard the huge bolt lock clang into place. She trudged over to the soft bed and lay down on top of the covers, staring up at the ceiling high above.

The whirlwind fairy tale was officially over. From now on, Paige was nothing but another prisoner.

"Just tell me again why this is a good idea," Leo said to Phoebe as they made their way along the crowded street toward St. John's Pub. "We're going to see the bad guy because . . . ?"

"Because we want him to trust us so he keeps us informed of his plans," Phoebe replied under her breath, looking around to make sure no one was following them or listening in. "He's going to hear about Corinne's arrest through the grapevine eventually. We were sent there to make sure everything went as planned. If we don't tell him about Corinne first, he's going to know something is up."

"Ah," Leo said. "So this is a preemptive move."

"Basically, yeah," Phoebe said, ducking into the pub. "Let's just hope it works."

"Sinjin's been waiting for you," the barmaid said as Phoebe and Leo stepped up to the bar. "I'll show you the way."

Phoebe glanced at Leo as they followed the woman down a hallway behind the bar to a closed door in the very back of the building. Sinjin had never met Piper, so she had stayed behind at the castle to keep Paige company, but at that moment, Phoebe wouldn't have minded having her sister and her fire power to back her up. Now that she was actually here, she was starting to feel a bit of her brother-in-law's trepidation. There was something about this Sinjin guy that made her very skin crawl.

Maybe it's the fact that he's plotting to murder thousands of innocent people, Phoebe thought wryly as they passed by four stocky guards in the hallway. *Yeah. That could be it.*

The barmaid paused and rapped on the door.

"Enter!" Sinjin's voice came through loud and clear.

The barmaid stepped aside and Leo opened the door, walking in first. Phoebe stepped in next to him as Sinjin looked up from a large roll of parchment that was stretched out on his desk. His dark eyes lit up when he saw his visitors, and he stood and walked around the desk to face them.

"Ah. My spies," he said, his thin lips curling

into a smirk. He placed his hands on his hips and looked them up and down. "I trust you have good news for me."

Leo and Phoebe exchanged a quick glance.

"I'm afraid not," Leo replied, causing Sinjin's eyes to darken.

"Well?" he snapped. "Is the girl dead or not?"

Phoebe tried to swallow, but her dry throat wouldn't allow it. She stifled a cough behind her hand as Sinjin's eyes slid over to her.

"Tell me what's happened now, before I lose patience and slit both your throats," Sinjin said, his tone as cordial as if he were welcoming them into his home rather than threatening to kill them.

"The girl you sent to do the job was caught and arrested," Leo said.

"What?" Sinjin exploded.

"She's in the dungeon right now," Phoebe added, finally recovering herself. "The king and queen are deciding on her punishment."

"This is unacceptable," Sinjin said, pacing around to the other side of the desk again. He pressed his fists into the hard surface of the wood and clenched his teeth. "Unacceptable!" he shouted.

With a huge roar, he suddenly swept everything off his desk with both arms. Papers went flying, a globe cracked into pieces on the floor, quills and bottles smashed against the far wall. The noise was so loud that three armed men came bursting in, their hands on their swords.

Phoebe jumped back, ready to fight, keeping her eyes on the weapons.

"Sir! Is everything all right in here?" one of the men asked, eyeing Leo and Phoebe.

"Fine! Leave us!" Sinjin shouted, catching his breath.

When the men didn't move, Sinjin lifted his right arm and swung it in a wide arc. "I said leave!"

There was a huge blast of white-hot power and the three huge guards were suddenly flung out as if they had been yanked from behind by some invisible force. Outside they crashed into the wall and took out a glass case full of metal plates and goblets. Phoebe's heart caught in her throat. The door slammed and she and Leo were left alone with Sinjin again. Alone with a psycho who was packing some serious magic.

"I should have known," Sinjin said slowly, glaring down at his now empty desk. "I should have known that I couldn't trust a mortal. Of course she was caught. She's nothing but a stupid, sniveling human."

Phoebe bit down on her tongue to keep from lashing out at Sinjin. A person could only take so much of this cretin without losing it, but she didn't want to suffer the same fate as the guards.

"We should probably go," Leo said, glancing at Phoebe.

She pushed herself away from the wall and

started for the door. They had learned nothing new, other than the fact that Sinjin was teetering on the edge, but they could always come back. She was sure that there would be a meeting later that night to regroup and come up with a new plan. The wedding, after all, was scheduled for the next day—Colin's birthday. If the loyalists were going to act, they had to act quickly. But for now, all Phoebe wanted to do was get away from Sinjin.

"Wait!" Sinjin said as soon as Leo's hand touched the doorknob. "Wait," he repeated more quietly. He rubbed his chin with his hand as he mulled something over. Phoebe's heart pounded with foreboding. Whatever was coming, it couldn't be good.

"It's up to you now," Sinjin said, finally looking them each in the eye.

Leo glanced at Phoebe, then met Sinjin's gaze. "What's up to us?" he asked.

"This wedding cannot proceed as planned. Our entire cause depends on it," Sinjin said. "But now that an attempt has been made on Lady Paige's life, they'll be fortifying the castle against further attacks."

"What does that have to do with us?" Phoebe said.

"Well, normally I would send in one of my most trusted men to do the job, but none of them will be getting anyone else past the royal family's security," Sinjin continued, growing excited as the plan formed itself more clearly in his mind. "But you two . . . you can come and go as you please, can you not?"

Phoebe's chest filled with dread and her breath started to come quick and shallow.

"You do work at the palace, don't you?" Sinjin asked Leo. "Isn't that what you told me yesterday?"

"Yes, but—"

"No. No buts," Sinjin said, waving a hand. "This is no time to be skittish, my friends. You are about to ascend to glory. You are about to become the saviors of Tarsina. You will go down in history as the people who changed our fate."

Phoebe and Leo fell quiet as Sinjin walked over to them, his boots clomping against the wooden floor. He paused in front of them, lifted his eyes, and grinned devilishly.

"You will bring me the head of the Lady Paige," he said. "You will do it, or you will die."

"All right! That's it! We're outta here!" Piper said, pushing herself up off the window seat in Paige's chamber. She flicked her fingers at Paige, who was sitting at the table, a large tome about the history of Tarsina open in front of her. "Come on, kiddo. Let's go."

"Piper, wait," Leo said.

"No. I'm not waiting. Not anymore," Piper replied. "I've had just about enough of this. Let's go. We're orbing home. These people are just going to have to take care of themselves."

When Paige didn't move, Piper grabbed her sister's hand and hauled her up. Paige tripped to her feet and quickly yanked her hand out of Piper's grasp.

"Piper, I'm not going anywhere," Paige said.

"Paige! Didn't you hear what they just said?" Piper demanded, gesturing at Phoebe and Leo. "Sinjin wants them to *kill* you! He wants them to bring him your *head*! I kind of like your head where it's always been. On your neck! Now let's go."

Paige took a few more steps away from Piper. Piper wished that she had been born with the power to orb. If she had it, she would have tackled Paige right then and there and kidnapped her back to the Manor.

"Okay, am I the only one thinking straight around here?" Piper asked, raising her hands and looking around at her family. "If you two don't go back there with Paige's head in a bag, this Sinjin guy is going to know you're not for real and he's going to send someone to kill *all* of you. Personally, I think we should know when to admit defeat."

"Piper, I made a promise to these people," Paige said. "Do you realize what's going to happen if I leave here? We're talking total death and destruction."

"Excuse me for saying this, but at the moment,

your death and destruction is the only thing I care about," Piper said. "Yours and my husband's and Phoebe's."

"Look, I hate to say this, Piper, but Paige is right," Leo said. "We can't let Tarsina be taken over by evil magic, which is what will happen if all the mortals die. Evil will have won out and it will slowly poison everything in this realm. The Elders think—"

"Like I really care what the Elders think right now," Piper said, bringing her hands to her head and sitting down on the edge of the bed. She had never felt so trapped, so helpless. Why couldn't Colin have just fallen in love with some magical girl from Tarsina? Hadn't he and his parents known about this curse their entire lives? What ever happened to a good old arranged marriage?

"Piper, Leo's right," Phoebe said gently, sitting down next to her. "If this place goes bad, it's going to seriously affect the balance of good and evil. And we all know we can't let that happen."

"So what's the plan, then?" Piper asked, dropping her hands. "What are we going to do, bring the man a papier-mâché head?"

Leo smirked. "Piper—"

"No, I'm serious, Leo," Piper said, standing again. "If we're going to stick it out here, we'd better come up with one hell of a plan to throw Sinjin off our trail. Because if we don't, at this point, I'm thinking I'll be going home alone."

Everyone in the room took a deep breath. They all knew that Piper was right. These loyalists were not going to stop until Paige was dead, one way or another.

"We need to come up with a way to fake him out," Piper said. "And we need to do it now."

Chapter Ten

The following morning the streets of Tarsina were alive with activity. Everyone knew that it was the prince's wedding day. Everyone knew that they were going to be saved. As Phoebe, Piper, and Leo walked down Kingston Road, spontaneous cheers could be heard from all over the city. Enticing scents wafted from many windows as people prepared for celebrations to be held that night. Bells rang out, children skipped along in their finest clothes. It was one big victory party.

Phoebe watched it all with a heavy heart. These people were so confident in Colin and Paige. They weren't even worried about what would happen if, for some reason, the wedding did not go off. She looked down at the small sack in her hands and tried to make herself breathe. In many ways, the fates of all these people depended on her and Leo executing their plan with Sinjin.

Unfortunately, it was not a foolproof plan.

"They all look so happy," Piper said, glancing at a group of people who were laughing and chatting over breakfast at an outdoor café. "Aren't they worried at all?"

"Maybe they're just trying to focus on the positive," Leo said.

"Yeah, well, I wish I could," Phoebe told them as they stepped onto the side street. St. John's Pub was a little farther down the block, its placard swinging slightly in the breeze. "Do you guys really think this is going to work?" she asked, lifting the sack.

"Well, it's all we've got," Piper said in a tone that didn't raise Phoebe's hopes at all. "Now remember, just try to get in and out as quickly as you can. I'll be outside the window of his office if anything goes wrong."

"Okay," Phoebe said with a nod as they paused in front of the pub.

"Be careful," Piper said.

She turned and slipped down the alley that led around the back of the building. Phoebe looked up at Leo and sighed.

"Let's get this over with," she said.

The barmaid seemed to be expecting them and sent them straight back to Sinjin's office. Phoebe's heart was pounding so hard she wanted to cover her chest with her hand. For the first time, there was no guard standing watch outside Sinjin's door. Phoebe wasn't sure if this was a good sign or a bad sign. Leo shrugged and knocked.

"Enter!" Sinjin called out.

"Here goes nothing," Phoebe said under her breath as they stepped inside.

The moment they were through the door, Phoebe understood why there had been no guard. All of Sinjin's top men were gathered in his office with him. Two stood in the corner with the man himself, their heads bent together in intense conversation. Another four milled about the room, talking in low voices and looking generally surly. Who knew what kinds of powers these men had? If anything went awry in here, Phoebe and Leo were toast.

"Ah! It's our guests of honor," Sinjin said, raising his chin as he stepped away from his cohorts.

Phoebe felt a little flutter of hope as Sinjin stood behind his desk. Behind him was the one dirt-smeared window in his office, and behind that somewhere was Piper, their major fire power.

Sinjin looked Phoebe and Leo over, and as he did so his eyes narrowed and the smile faded from his face. Finally his eyes fell on the burlap bag in Phoebe's hand.

"That doesn't seem big enough to be the head of a lady," he said, eliciting a laugh from his men.

Phoebe could already feel them closing in on her from behind. The air in the office grew warmer and suddenly everything felt tight—

constricted. All the hairs on the back of her neck stood on end.

"So where is it?" Sinjin asked. "Where is the head you were supposed to bring me? Our time is running short."

Phoebe cleared her throat. "Well, you know how magical beings are," she said, trying to act nonchalant. "We did kill her, but before we could remove her head, she disappeared in a swirl of white orbs."

"Yeah, just like that," Leo added. "She was just gone."

Sinjin nodded slowly, as if he was thinking this over. He glanced at the bag again. "Then what proof have you brought me that she is, in fact, dead?"

Phoebe glanced at Leo, and he nodded ever so slightly. Fingers shaking, Phoebe opened the bag and pulled out the queen's rune. She held it up high and a couple of the men behind her gasped. Phoebe was buoyed by the reaction. They had been hoping that Tarsinians would understand the significance of the necklace— that they would know that the queen always gave it to the princess-to-be and that no one in their right mind would remove it.

"You see?" Phoebe said, laying the necklace on the desk. "Lady Paige never would have parted with the sacred rune if she were still alive."

Sinjin reached for the rune and reverently

touched the largest stone with his fingertips. He picked it up, draped the heavy necklace over one hand, and clasped the stone with his other. For a moment he closed his eyes as if he were praying. Phoebe held her breath.

Just let us go, she thought. *Just take this as proof and let us go.*

Finally, Sinjin opened his eyes again and glared directly at Phoebe. She swallowed back a gasp. This was not the look of a person who was pleased.

"You are both such fools," he said through his teeth. "Did you really think you could come in here and pass yourselves off as loyalists when clearly you know nothing about Tarsina?"

Phoebe gulped. This was not good. This was very, very not good.

"Who are you?" Sinjin demanded. "Where did you come from?"

"I don't understand," Phoebe said, trying to keep her cool.

"Obviously not," Sinjin said. "Let me clear it up for you. Everyone in Tarsina knows that the queen's rune cannot be removed from the wearer's neck by anyone but the wearer herself. Everyone also knows that if the Lady Paige were indeed dead, as you claim, this necklace would have automatically returned to the neck of the lady who last wore it. This rune would be gracing the neck of my sister, the queen, right now. It would be back where it rightfully belongs!"

Oh God. Oh God, this is bad, Phoebe thought, taking a step back. *Wait a minute . . . his* what?

"Your sister?" she said, breathless.

"Yes, my sister. Queen Ramona of Tarsina. Her Majesty in whose honor we fight. My sister who, above all, wishes for our ancestor's curse to come true. For our kingdom to reclaim its purity," Sinjin ranted, his eyes on fire as he clutched the rune.

Phoebe couldn't believe what she was hearing. Colin's mother was behind all this? The woman who had tripled the guards on Paige's door? The woman who seemed so determined to make sure her son wed a magical being? How could this be? How could she do this to her own people?

"My sister," Sinjin continued, "in whose name you will now be put to death."

In one swift motion the guards advanced on Leo and Phoebe.

"Piper!" Leo shouted at the top of his lungs.

Leo grabbed Phoebe and shielded her as the window behind Sinjin exploded, along with some of the wall, throwing him forward into his desk. A few of the guards were knocked out, and the others were so stunned that it gave Phoebe and Leo just enough time to scramble through the hole and out into the alleyway.

"What happened?" Piper asked.

"We'll tell you later. If we live that long," Phoebe said.

Then Leo grabbed them both and orbed them out of the fray.

Paige stared at her reflection in the gilt-framed mirror above her dressing table as Marissa, one of the many maids assigned to cater to her every wish, brushed her hair slowly and methodically. Her head was full of a million and one concerns, so full that she felt as if she could barely hold it up. At the same time her pulse was pounding with a mixture of excitement and fear unlike anything she had ever felt before. It was her wedding day, and part of her wished she were anywhere but here.

"Marissa? Do you think I could get just a few minutes to myself?" Paige asked.

"Certainly, miss," Marissa said, stepping back and dropping into a little curtsy.

She pocketed the hairbrush and snapped her fingers at the other girls who were all working on the wedding gown and laying out Paige's slippers and veil. They gathered up into a little clump and hustled out of the room together, giggling and talking the whole way.

Paige glanced at the clock on the wall and wondered how the meeting with Sinjin was going. The longer her sisters and Leo took, the more nervous she became. A quick return would have meant that Sinjin had been fooled. As the minutes ticked by it was more and more possible that Phoebe, Piper, and Leo had been found out and captured.

They may even be . . . dead, Paige thought, staring into her own eyes, not even wanting to think it. But no, it wasn't possible. If her sisters were dead, she would know. She would feel it. She was almost positive of this fact.

Paige took a deep breath and pulled down the scarf that was hiding her bare neck. She had covered herself up, knowing that the maids would notice that the queen's necklace was missing. Even though she had worn it for only a few days, the absence of its weight was obvious to her. Paige had no idea how she was going to walk down the aisle without it. The queen would most likely throw a fit when she saw that her heirloom was missing. Maybe Phoebe and Leo would find a way to bring it back.

Her eyes flicked to the clock once again. Two minutes had passed. Two long minutes.

"Come on, you guys. Where are you?" Paige whispered.

The doors behind Paige flew open and she whirled around with a relieved grin. But it wasn't Phoebe, Piper, and Leo walking into her room, it was the queen. This was odd. Usually Luka announced her visitors—even the queen herself. But Paige didn't have enough time to dwell on his faux pas. She was too busy scrambling for the scarf and covering her neck with it again.

"Good morning, Paige," the queen said with one of her trademark tight smiles. "You look beautiful."

"Thank you, Your Majesty," Paige said. "Have you seen Colin? How is he?"

"He's fine, dear," the queen said. "Just fine."

The queen walked over to Paige and placed her hand on top of her head like a loving mother. Paige would have found it an almost sweet gesture if the woman's hand hadn't been so frigidly cold and hard.

"It's such a shame," the queen said. "You would have made such a spectacular bride."

Paige looked up at the queen, her brow knitting. Her heart skipped a troubled beat. "Would have made?"

"Yes. If you were actually getting married today," the queen said.

Then, before Paige could even blink, the woman's eyes swirled and darkened to an inky black. Paige had just enough time to register that this could not be a good thing, before she was completely and soundly knocked out.

The moment Piper appeared in Paige's chamber, she knew something was wrong. It was too silent. Too motionless. It was not the room of a person who was about to be married in the biggest celebration of the century. She whipped around, checking the entire room, but no one was there.

"This can't be right. Where the hustle? Where's the bustle?" Piper said.

"The queen must have already been here," Phoebe said. "She must have gotten to Paige."

"The queen?" Piper asked. "The queen is in on this?"

"At least according to Sinjin," Leo said.

"Yeah," Phoebe responded, heading for the door. "Apparently no one is what they seem around here."

"Ooh. I knew I didn't trust that pointy little witch," Piper said, her adrenaline pumping.

Phoebe whipped open the heavy doors and a guard fell right into the room at her feet.

"Oh my God," Phoebe said, dropping to her knees. She pressed her fingers to Luka's throat and sighed. "He's alive," she said with obvious relief.

Piper stepped over him and out into the hallway. Together they checked over Luka and the five other guards. They had all been rendered unconscious.

"This is not good," Piper said, her pulse racing through her veins. "You know what I want to find out right about now? Whether or not *Colin* is what he seems."

"Let's go," Leo said.

"What happened here?"

Piper turned to find Colin himself rushing up to them. His eyes were wide with surprise and fear as he took in the guards. If he was in on the plot, if he was acting, he was doing an amazing job.

"Paige? Is Paige all right?" he asked, his face going ashen.

"No, she's not all right. She's missing," Piper told him. "And apparently your mother had something to do with it."

"My mother? How dare you say—"

"Think about it, Colin," Phoebe said. "Who else would have access to Paige today? Luka knew that no one was supposed to be allowed to see her but us. Who could get by them but a very powerful witch? Someone who normally has free rein to walk around the castle?"

Colin looked down at Luka's slack face. "There must be some other explanation," he said.

"Then why don't we go see your mother and find out?" Piper suggested.

Clenching his jaw, Colin gave a firm nod and turned on his heel. He led them all down the hall to the royal chamber where his parents had been holding court all week. Piper felt a wave of foreboding wash over her as they stepped through the open doors. This room, which had been full of courtiers and maids and musicians ever since their arrival, was now, like Paige's, completely devoid of life.

"Father!" Colin shouted.

Piper didn't even see the lump of velvet robes on the floor until Colin was kneeling beside it. He reached out and turned his father over onto his back. There was a horrible gash across his stomach and blood everywhere. Piper had seen a lot of gruesome sights in her life, but for a split second she had to turn her face away from this one. The king had always been so kind to them. He didn't deserve to die such an awful death.

"Father!" Colin cried again, bowing his head over the king's body.

Leo raced over to them and fell to his knees. He placed his hands over the king's wound and instantly everything started to glow.

"He's still alive," Leo said.

"Oh, thank God," Colin whispered.

"Don't worry," Leo said. "I've got him."

Piper held her breath as her husband worked his magic. A moment later the blood was gone, the gash was healed, and the king sat up. He gasped a few times and looked around himself perplexed, but none the worse for wear.

"Father! Are you all right?" Colin asked, hugging his dad with both arms around his neck.

"What happened?" the king asked.

"Someone tried to kill you," Leo told him. "Do you remember what happened?"

"No, I . . . I . . . ," The king struggled to stand, and Colin helped him to his feet. The second he was up again, his face went white and his knees buckled. Leo sprang forward and with Colin's help managed to get the king over to his throne. "Oh my God. Colin. It was your mother," the king said, his eyes wide.

"Father . . . no," Colin said breathlessly.

"Son . . . I'm so, so sorry," the king said, clearly in anguish.

Colin knelt at his father's feet, took the older man's hands in his own, and gazed up at him. "Sorry for what, father? What's going on?"

"It's your mother. I didn't know. I had no idea . . . ," the king said. "She . . . she did this to me. I tried to stop her, but—"

"No," Colin replied with tears in his eyes. "No. She couldn't have."

The king grasped his son's arms and looked him right in the eyes. "Colin, it's true. Your mother is a loyalist. She sent Corinne to woo you because she thought you would never be able to marry another when you were already in love. She underestimated you, though."

"She would never do that," Colin said, shaking his head.

"Colin, you have to believe me now," his father said firmly. "Look into my eyes. You would know if I was lying to you."

Colin did as his father said and looked directly into his eyes, searching. After a long moment, he dropped his head and covered his face with both hands. Piper knew that Colin had finally seen the truth. She knew that his heart was shattering.

"You have to be strong now," his father said. "You have to save Paige. You have to save your kingdom."

"This doesn't make any sense," Colin said weakly. "I can't believe it."

"You have to believe it, Colin. You have to accept it," his father told him. "Your mother has taken Paige, and they're going to kill her. If you don't find them first, they're going to kill her, and the curse will be fulfilled."

Chapter Eleven

"**She's still** alive," Leo said, opening his eyes.

"Oh, thank God. Let's go get her." Piper grabbed Leo's hand. All she could think about was getting to her sister. They had no plan for what to do after they freed her, but just then Piper didn't care. The only thing that mattered was making sure Paige was safe.

"Wait! I want to come with you!" Colin said, stepping away from his father's side for the first time.

"No, Colin. You can't," Phoebe said. "Wherever they took Paige, she's probably being guarded by the loyalists. Who knows what they might do if they get desperate? They may kill both of you."

"No. My mother would never let that happen," Colin said.

"You also thought she would never hurt your father," Piper pointed out grimly. "Let us go get

Paige. You guys find the magistrate who's supposed to marry you and bring him back here to the throne room. We'll get Paige here and we can get this over with."

"Good idea," Phoebe said. "You don't need a big wedding, you just need to say the vows, right?"

"Right," Colin said, swallowing hard.

"Okay. We'll be back soon with your bride," Piper told him. Then she held on to her husband as he orbed them out.

Seconds later Piper found herself blinking in absolute darkness, trying to find something to focus on.

"Where are we?" she whispered, clutching Leo's hand.

"It's freezing. It must be some kind of basement," he said, his mouth very close to her ear.

Finally Piper's eyes adjusted and she could make out the outline of a door to her right. She turned around and saw a wash of white cloth curled up in the corner. Piper squinted and could just make out an arm. A slim, pale arm.

"Oh no, Leo. It's Paige," Piper said, rushing over to her sister.

She crouched on the floor and pulled Paige away from the cold, hard basement wall. Her sister's head lolled to the side, and Piper gently turned Paige's face so that her cheek was resting against Piper's chest. Her skin felt slick and bloodless.

"Paige? Paige, sweetie, wake up," Piper whispered, patting Paige's cheek lightly. There was no response. "Leo?" Piper asked, her voice scared and pleading.

Leo knelt on the floor and placed his hands on either side of Paige's head. "I think she's under some kind of spell," he said.

"Can you do anything?" Piper asked.

"Hang on."

Leo closed his eyes and Piper heard his breath growing labored. Suddenly his hands started to glow, casting an eerie but warm light over Paige's ·pale features. Piper glanced at the door, worried that the light might attract someone's attention. But when she felt Paige start to move in her arms, she ceased to care. One crisis at a time.

"Piper?" Paige asked groggily.

"Yeah, it's me," Piper said, hugging her tight. "You're gonna be okay."

At that moment the door to the cell was shoved open and three guards came bursting in. Piper was about to grab Leo so he could orb them out, but the first guard was quicker. He took Leo by the shoulder and slammed him back into the wall, separating him from Paige and Piper.

"Paige, orb yourself out of here," Piper said, standing up.

A few weak orbs appeared around Paige's body but quickly disappeared. Apparently she was too weak for that just yet.

"You're going to be sorry you ever came to Tarsina," one of the guards growled at Piper, baring his scraggly, yellow teeth.

"Believe me, buddy, I already am," Piper said. Then she lifted her hands and blew him to pieces.

"Piper!" Leo cried.

She whirled around and saw that Leo was desperately fighting off the other two guards. He shoved one across the room and took a sharp jab across the jaw from the second. Piper spun around and blasted the first guard to bits before he could even scramble to his feet. Two down, one to go.

Then Piper heard it—the commotion outside the door. From the sounds of the shouting voices and the hurried footsteps, the explosions had caught the attention of a few more lurking loyalists. Piper rolled her shoulders back and turned toward the door, bracing herself for a major battle. She was going to get her sisters and her husband out of this godforsaken place, or die trying.

Outside the castle Phoebe and Colin ran across the courtyard as the skies overhead began to darken. For the first time since Phoebe had arrived in Tarsina, thick clouds rolled across the pristine blue sky, blocking out the ever-shining sun. A chill skittered down her spine as Colin turned a corner and headed for a small stone cottage. All around them guards and courtiers raced for cover. A man in the royal armor shouted instructions to a few petrified women, a couple of whom were in tears. No one seemed to notice that the crown prince of the kingdom was racing by them.

"What's happening?" Phoebe asked, checking the sky above.

"It's the curse," Colin said. "The hour of my birth is approaching. We don't have much time. Why didn't I see this coming? I always knew my mother adhered to the old traditions, but I never thought . . . Why didn't I realize she was a loyalist?"

"Don't blame yourself, Colin," Phoebe said, reaching out to lay a comforting hand on his arm. "Everything's going to be—"

Suddenly the path in front of Phoebe disappeared, and she was overcome by a vivid premonition that blocked out everything around her. She stopped in her tracks and concentrated, taking in every detail. An old woman Phoebe didn't recognize lay on a bed in a small room. She was clearly weak and scared—possibly taking her last breaths. Standing next to her bed, clutching her hand, was Corinne, and hovering behind them was Colin. Phoebe saw herself handing a spell to the old woman and watching as she recited it. And then, just as suddenly as the premonition had come, it was gone, and Phoebe was back in the real world, staring at a very concerned Colin.

"Phoebe? Are you all right?"

Phoebe was suddenly overcome by a certainty so clear that her entire body was warmed from the inside out.

"You're smiling. Why are you smiling?" Colin asked her.

"I think I know a way that you can marry Corinne and still save the kingdom," Phoebe told him.

"What?" Colin said. "You're telling me this now?"

"Well, I didn't know until now," Phoebe said, grabbing his hand and looking up into his eyes. "Listen to me. Is there an old woman in your and Corinne's life? Someone who's sick? Maybe dying."

Colin's brow furrowed and Phoebe knew that he was trying to figure out what any of this had to do with him and the curse—why she was wasting precious time.

"Corinne's grandmother," he said finally. "She's been sick for weeks."

"This grandmother," Phoebe said. "Is she a pure magical being?"

"Yes," Colin said. "She's the one in Corinne's family who married a mortal. But I don't understand—"

"We have to get Corinne together with her grandmother," Phoebe said as thunder crashed overhead. "We have to do it now."

Colin glanced over his shoulder at the

cottage where the magistrate lived. Outside the castle gates, people were screaming in fear. A single raindrop hit Phoebe's cheek so hard it stung.

Finally Colin turned to Phoebe and nodded. He had decided to trust her. "Okay," he said. "I just hope you know what you're doing."

Me too, Phoebe thought as it started to rain in earnest.

"Let's go."

Phoebe held on to the wall as she followed Colin down the winding stone staircase that led to Corinne's dungeon far beneath the castle. They had left the aging magistrate at the top of the steps at Colin's suggestion, and now Phoebe understood why. She could barely see where she was going, and each step was more treacherous than the last. If the man had come with them, this would have been a very slow descent.

"The magistrate seemed confused by our whole switching brides thing," Phoebe said. "Not that I blame him, but is he going to be all right?"

"Don't worry. He'll marry me to whomever I ask," Colin replied. "He's a good man. There's not a loyalist bone in him."

"Who goes there?" a deep voice bellowed the moment Colin reached the ground.

"It's Prince Colin. Stand down," Colin said authoritatively.

"Colin?" Corinne's voice croaked from somewhere in the dungeon.

A skeletal man appeared from the shadows and stepped in Colin's path. He looked like the Grim Reaper himself. Over his shoulder Phoebe saw Corinne chained to the wall, her body hanging limply, straining her thin arms.

"I'm sorry, Your Highness, but your mother the queen has forbid me to let you see the prisoner," the guard said.

"My mother the queen is a traitor and a coward," Colin said, lifting his chin.

The guard's eyes flashed with anger. "I can't tell you how sorry I am you just said that."

In one swift motion he yanked a knife from his belt and lunged at Colin. The prince jumped out of the way and Phoebe hit the guard with a roundhouse kick to the gut. The guard dropped the knife and staggered back against the wall. Phoebe was about to finish him off when a fireball appeared above his palm. She jumped back, and Colin stepped between her and the guard.

"Drop it," he demanded.

The guard did as he was told. "Prince Colin, I have my orders," he said almost pleadingly.

"I know," Colin told him. "I understand."

Without another word Colin stepped forward and waved his hand in front of the guard's face. Instantly the man's eyes went blank and he stood up again. Phoebe watched cautiously as the guard walked over to the table in the corner and sat down, pulling a book toward him. Much to Phoebe's amazement, the guard just sat there, reading by candlelight, while Colin picked the keys off his belt and raced over to Corinne.

"What did you do to him?" Phoebe asked.

"That's my power," Colin said over his shoulder. "I can make people see whatever I want them to see. Right now that man has no idea we're here."

"Wow. That's some power," Phoebe said, thinking of all the damage Colin could do with a skill like that. He could rob banks without anyone being the wiser. He could sneak into people's rooms and watch their every move. He could basically render himself invisible.

"Yeah. That's why I almost never use it," Colin said.

"I can't believe you're here," Corinne said to him as he unlocked her chains. She fell into Colin's arms, clearly weak and emotionally spent. "Colin, I am so, so sorry. I know it's probably impossible, but if you could ever find a way to forgive me—"

"I know. It's okay." Colin planted a kiss on her cheek and another on her forehead. Corinne seemed to go slack with joy and relief. "Corinne, I love you," Colin said, steadying her. "I always have. But we've no time for this now. We have to get to your house."

He walked her over to Phoebe, who ducked under Corinne's arm so they could both help her up the stairs.

"My house? But why?" Corinne asked.

"It's a long story," Phoebe told her. "We'll fill you in on the way."

The trek up the stairs was long and arduous. Corinne explained that she hadn't eaten since she had been taken prisoner, so she had to stop every twenty steps or so to catch her breath and gather her strength. Finally, Colin lifted her in his arms and carried her up the last few rotations of the spiral staircase. Corinne buried her face in the crook between his neck and his shoulder, clinging to him as if her life depended on it.

Out on the street, people were huddled together against the driving rain, praying and crying. The loyalists had come out in full force to celebrate their victory. Looters broke into businesses and carried out everything from food to furniture, whooping it up and laughing with glee in the faces of the mortals who were about to die.

"This is sick," Phoebe said as she and the magistrate followed Colin through the mud and muck. "What's wrong with these people?"

"The moment this is over I'm finding a way to bring understanding and tolerance to my people," Colin promised, clutching Corinne to him. "This country cannot exist like this anymore."

"Well, at least no one's paying attention to us," Phoebe said as a band of young men raced by, cheering and shouting. "Where is Corinne's house, anyway?"

"It's right down here," Colin said, turning a corner.

The street ahead was lined with small, quaint cottages, some shut up tight with smoke billowing from the chimneys, some with doors open to the streets. A little girl sat on the front step of one of the houses, bawling her eyes out. Phoebe wondered where her parents were. She wondered how so many of these people could just sit inside their houses and wait for the curse to sweep away their neighbors. But then, what could they do? If the royal family couldn't stop the curse, these regular, run-of-the-mill witches probably felt there was no way for them to help. All at once, Phoebe felt anew the real evil of this curse. It rendered everyone helpless. It took free will right out of their hands.

Colin stopped in front of one of the closed-up houses and nodded at the door. Phoebe found it unlocked and stepped inside. The front room was cozy and lined with packed bookshelves from floor to ceiling. A table and chairs stood near the window, and in the far corner was a fireplace alight with a crackling fire. Corinne's father sat in front of the flames with a pretty, middle-aged woman who looked like an older version of Corinne. They turned around as Phoebe and the others stepped inside, and their eyes widened with joy when they saw Corinne. Richmond helped his wife to her feet and they both rushed forward.

"Thank God you're all right," Corinne's mother said, enveloping Corinne in a hug the moment Colin placed her feet on the ground.

Her father hugged her next and looked at Colin. "It's started, hasn't it?"

"Yes. But we're going to stop it," Phoebe said. She took Corinne's hand. "Where's your grandmother's room?"

"Through there," Corinne said, pointing at a door at the back of the room.

"Let's just hope this works," Phoebe said, leading the group into the small bedroom. "What's her name?" Phoebe asked, one hand on the doorknob.

"Misha," Corinne's father answered. "What's all this about?"

"We're going to save this place," Phoebe said, determined.

They walked into Misha's room, and Phoebe found the woman just as she had seen her in her premonition. Frail and thin, Misha lay in the center of her bed, her long white hair fanned out on one side of her face. She turned her head as her visitors entered, and her thin lips spread into a smile when she saw Corinne.

"Grandma," Corinne said, dropping to her knees at the side of the bed.

She hugged her grandmother, who placed a bony hand on her granddaughter's cheek. "I was hoping to see you again," Misha said.

A single tear spilled onto Corinne's cheek.

"Grandma, this is Phoebe," Corinne said, gesturing over her shoulder. "She wants to do a spell. She thinks it'll help stop the curse."

Misha's eyes focused on Phoebe, who stepped forward and leaned down over the bed.

"Misha, I want to try to transfer your powers to Corinne. I've rewritten a power-switching spell that my sisters and I once used and I think it'll work," Phoebe said gently. "I believe that if Corinne has your powers, she can marry Colin and stop the curse."

"But you won't have your powers anymore, Grandma," Corinne said, grasping her grandmother's hand. "Is that okay with you?"

"Oh, Corinne, of course," Misha said. "You know I love you both," she added, looking at Colin. "And you know I'd do anything for this kingdom. I won't be needing them much longer anyway."

Corinne closed her eyes as a few more tears spilled out, but she nodded and managed to smile. "Okay. Phoebe, what do we need to do?"

"Do you have a pad and pen?" Phoebe asked Corinne's mother.

"Sure," she replied. She left the room and came back a moment later with the tools. Phoebe scrawled out the spell on the top page and ripped it free, handing it to Misha.

"Okay, now hold hands and look into each other's eyes," Phoebe said, walking to the other side of the bed. Corinne clasped Misha's free hand in hers and gazed at her grandmother, smiling bravely. "Now, Misha, all you have to do is read the spell."

Misha nodded and squinted down at the page.

> *What's mine is yours.*
> *My power is thine.*
> *Let my magic cross the line.*
> *I offer up my gift to share.*
> *Send my powers through the air.*

Corinne looked up at Phoebe. "Did it work?"

"Go outside," Misha said weakly. "Give it a try."

Corinne scrambled to her feet, leaned over, and gave her grandmother a quick kiss. Then she raced out of the room and into the street. Phoebe, Colin, Corinne's parents, and the magistrate followed. The sky was as black as pitch now, the clouds hovering so low they seemed to be rolling down the street in front of them.

"What's her grandmother's power?" Phoebe shouted at Colin to be heard over the rain, the thunder, and the shouting of the desperate people all around them.

"Creating light in the darkness," Colin replied.

Well, that should come in handy right about now, Phoebe thought.

Corinne raised her arm to the sky and suddenly a beam of light exploded from her palm, burning a hole in the clouds. A patch of bright blue sky shone through and a few people on the street pointed up and gasped, hoping it meant the end of the storm.

"It worked!" Corinne cried. She reached out and grasped Colin's hand. "Let's do this!"

"Magistrate?" Phoebe said, stepping back. "Do your stuff. Just . . . do it quickly."

"I see your point," the magistrate said as water dripped from his beard and plastered his hair to his face. "Prince Colin, do you take Corinne Van Den Pelt to be your wife, to love and to cherish from now until the end of time?"

A stiff, driving wind blasted down the lane, nearly knocking the magistrate off his feet. Phoebe caught him and steadied him in front of the couple, all of them blinking against the rain.

"I do!" Colin shouted, gripping Corinne with all his might.

"Good!" the magistrate said. "Do you, Corinne Van Den Pelt take Prince Colin to be your husband, to love and to cherish from now until the end of time?"

"I do!" Corinne yelled.

"I now pronounce you husband and wife! You may kiss the bride!" the magistrate said.

Colin pulled Corinne to him and kissed her shivering lips. They were both grinning as they pulled apart and looked up at the sky, waiting for it to clear. Waiting for the wind to stop and the rain to dry and the clouds to part.

But nothing happened. If anything, the storm grew worse.

"What's going on?" Corinne cried.

"It has to be the powers," her father replied. "You have them now, but you still aren't a pure magical being."

"What?" Phoebe cried, clenching her hands into fists. "This is insane! I saw this in a premonition! It should have worked!"

"Well, something went wrong," Richmond said. "And we now have less than twenty minutes."

"All right, that's it," Phoebe said. She looked up into the rain and called out at the top of her lungs, "Leo! Leo! We need a Plan C!"

Chapter Twelve

As guard after guard came rushing into Paige's cell, Piper stood in the center of the room and picked them off like she was playing some monotonous video game. Each one cried out as she hit them with her fire power, but the guys behind them didn't seem to take notice. They just kept coming and coming.

"Leo! I can't keep doing this forever," Piper called, opening her hands and firing at another guard.

"I know!" Leo said, gathering Paige up in his arms. "And Phoebe's calling me. Let's just get out of here."

"You're not going anywhere," a sinister voice promised.

Then, with a blast of heat, Leo was flung clear across the room, where he slammed into the stone wall. He fell to the ground and groaned in pain, wincing as his hand held his back. Every cell in Piper's body boiled as she turned to face Sinjin.

"You know, I'm a little sick of you people," Sinjin said with fake consternation. "What right is it of yours to come to my kingdom and start messing with my plans?"

"This kingdom doesn't belong to you," Piper said. "It belongs to the people you're trying to murder."

"Now, now," Sinjin said, stepping toward her. "I'm not trying to murder *all* of them, just the impure ones. Is that so wrong?"

From the corner of her eye, Piper saw Leo crawling toward Paige. A few more guards stepped into the room and gathered around Sinjin. They didn't even notice Leo's movements. When Sinjin was in their midst, all eyes were focused on him. Piper, for one, had had just about enough of this guy and his little speeches.

"You know what's wrong? You thinking you can take me on," Piper said, putting on her best cocky face.

Sinjin's expression clouded over. Piper had the feeling that he wasn't used to being challenged.

"You're no match for my power, girl," he said.

"Well let's find out," Piper said. "'Cause I'm getting a little sick of you, too."

With a maniacal sneer, Sinjin raised his arm to toss Piper, but she was too fast for him. One flick of her fingers and Sinjin, just like all the idiotic guards who had come before him, was gone. In the end he was nothing more than a run-of-the-mill bad witch. Easy as pie to vanquish.

His followers froze in disbelief, their leader gone in a flash. Piper looked at them and smiled.

"I don't know about you, but that seemed almost anticlimactic," she said.

Then, just as their fury set in and they started to charge her, she dove to the floor, grabbed Leo's arm, and orbed out of the cell with him and Paige. When she materialized again, she was standing in the middle of a muddy street being pelted by driving rain. All around her people screamed and ran and cried. Phoebe, Colin, Corinne, and a few others stood in front of them, shivering in the cold.

"What's going on?" Leo asked.

He placed Paige on her feet and she managed to stand without help. She still looked weak, but she wasn't dazed or confused anymore. Her eyes were clear and full of fear.

"It's happening," Corinne said, looking baffled and scared. "The curse. It's actually happening."

"I can't believe I let it get this far," Colin said, clinging to Corinne. "I've doomed my own people."

"This isn't over yet," Piper told him, trying to keep the terror out of her own voice. "Phoebe, what are you guys doing out here?"

"I got a premonition and thought I had

figured out a way for Corinne and Colin to marry, but it didn't work," Phoebe explained, water dripping from her ears and chin.

"We only have fifteen minutes," Colin shouted over a huge cheer from a nearby house.

"It's hopeless," Corinne said, her bottom lip quivering. "It's over. We're . . . we're really going to die."

A mother raced by, cradling a baby in her arms and dragging a toddler by the hand. Somewhere nearby children were crying and a woman's voice was raised in prayer. Piper's hands clenched into fists, and she was overcome by a rush of pure adrenaline. This couldn't happen. It wouldn't. Not on her watch.

"We have to get back to the castle," she said. She turned and started to walk away, expecting the rest of them to fall in line behind her. "We are going to stop this stupid curse once and for all."

"But how?" Colin cried. "We've tried everything."

Piper paused and turned. Her hair clung to her face and neck and her feet sank into the thick mud. Chaos reigned all around her and the very sky looked as if it was about to swallow them whole. But Piper felt none of it. Saw none of it.

She looked Colin in the eye and an overwhelming calm came over her. "We haven't tried the Power of Three."

• • •

Phoebe, Piper, and Paige sat at a table in the throne room at the very center of the palace, huddled together against the freezing cold. Wind whipped through the open windows, blowing Phoebe's hair back from her face and covering her skin with goose bumps. Apparently the people of Tarsina had never heard of windowpanes or shutters, but why would they have? Until this day, they had never needed them.

All around them guards and maids and stable hands and nobles raced about, working at the Charmed Ones' orders. A large space had been cleared on the stone floor and all the wall hangings and curtains had been removed from the area. Workers were bringing in every artifact that had belonged to the old queen and placing them in a pile in the middle of the room. So far they had hauled in an ancient-looking throne, a rolled-up tapestry, a few pieces of jewelry, and a huge painting of the ancestor herself. The painting had been placed on the side of the pile and faced Phoebe and her sisters as they worked. Every now and then Phoebe found herself staring into the old queen's eyes. There seemed to be no color in them. They were black as coal.

"Okay, I think we have it," Paige said, passing a piece of paper over to Phoebe. "What do you think? Are the words powerful enough?"

Phoebe tore her gaze away from the evil

queen and looked down at the spell. This was going to be the biggest cleansing ritual of all time and they only had one shot at it. They had to get the wording just right.

She read it over and nodded. "It's good," she said. "Now all we have to do is hope that it's good enough to expel an unexpellable curse."

There was a crash in the hallway and moments later two dozen men and women, including Colin, Corinne, and Corinne's parents staggered in, carrying a huge bed among them. The headboard was carved with flowers and vines that curled around four long swords that had been chiseled into the posts. Right in the center was the symbol of Tarsina, the swirling *T* that was also tattooed on Colin's arm. The men placed the bed next to the other artifacts and went about chopping its gorgeous wooden frame to bits with axes and saws. They cheered and cried out as they worked, expelling years of pent-up fear and resentment and anger. Each piece that was chopped free was placed around the pile of artifacts, all the better to send everything up in flames.

A blinding flash of lightning lit the room, accompanied by a blast of thunder so loud that it shook the foundations of the castle. Everyone in the room turned to look out the windows. It was as if night had fallen outside, even though it was only four o'clock in the afternoon.

"We have two minutes," Colin shouted. "If we're ever going to do this, the time is now."

Phoebe stood up, hoping no one could tell that her knees were shaking. She clutched the spell in her hand and looked at her sisters.

"Come on," she said. "Let's save a kingdom."

Every magical being in the castle gathered around the pile of the evil queen's belongings and clasped hands. The castle shook beneath their feet. Corinne stood along the wall, huddled with her mother and the other mortals who had bravely stuck around to help the cause. Richmond brought a lit torch in from the hallway and handed it to Paige. She took a deep breath and looked around at the scared, yet determined faces of the witches around her.

"Everybody ready?" she asked.

Colin and his father, along with Luka and dozens of strangers, nodded. They watched hopefully as Paige stepped forward and set fire to the tapestry and wood. She touched the flame to the framed painting of the evil queen and clenched her jaw as she tossed the torch on top of the pile. She reclaimed her spot in the circle, grasping the hands of her two sisters. Smoke billowed up from the pile, swirling toward the high ceiling and whipping around in the wind.

"Let's do this," Paige said. "We'll recite the

spell once and then you guys come in," she shouted, directing the others. "We'll repeat it as many times as we have to. Okay?"

There was a deafening rumble and the floor tilted, nearly knocking a couple of people off their feet. The circle wasn't broken, however, and everyone simply held on a little tighter.

Paige squeezed her sisters' hands and they recited the spell together.

> *Curse of evil, born of fear,*
> *no longer will you settle here.*
> *We call upon our ancient power*
> *in this darkest, bleakest hour.*
> *Expel this evil, expel the night.*
> *Bring us peace, bring us light.*

The people of Tarsina joined in as the Charmed Ones recited their spell once more. They shouted to be heard over the raging storm and howling wind. They shouted through their terror. In one voice, they screamed in the face of the curse that had haunted them for the better part of a century.

> *Curse of evil, born of fear,*
> *no longer will you settle here. . . .*

The doors to the throne room crashed open and Colin's mother stormed in, her black makeup streaming down her face, her blond hair hanging in knots around her shoulders.

"What do you think you're doing?" she cried as a half dozen of her loyalist guards tromped in, gathering around her. "Colin! Get away from there! You can't do this! You can't!"

Everyone ignored her and continued the spell.

> *We call upon our ancient power*
> *in this darkest, bleakest hour. . . .*

The queen's eyes fell on the smoldering artifacts in the center of the circle. At that moment everything was suddenly enveloped in a swirling tornado of black smoke. Paige narrowed her eyes as the tornado whipped into a frenzy, spinning faster and faster, throwing silt and dirt and ash in all directions. She grasped her sisters' hands, holding on for dear life.

"Don't break the circle!" she shouted. "Everyone hold on!"

At Paige's words the queen rushed forward and grabbed her son's and husband's hands, trying desperately to tear them apart. Then, out of nowhere, a beam of white light hit the queen directly in the chest, flinging her across the room, where she slammed into the wall and fell into a heap on the floor. Paige caught a glimpse of Corinne standing with her arm outstretched toward the crumpled queen.

Expel this evil, expel the night.
Bring us peace, bring us light.

The tornado whipped Paige's hair into her eyes. Dirt and debris flew everywhere. A few people crouched to the floor to protect themselves, but continued to cling to one another, never breaking the circle.

"What's happening?" Piper shouted over the noise. "Is it working?"

"I don't know!" Phoebe shouted back.

And then the wind just stopped. The tornado disappeared in a poof of smoke. The room grew quiet and still. Outside, the clouds started to break and a weak ray of sunshine shone through. Paige looked down at the space in the center of the circle. Every last scrap of the evil queen's junk was gone.

"We did it," Paige said, then glanced around for confirmation. "Did we do it?"

"It's over," Colin said with a huge grin. Dirt and grime streaked his face, but his elation shone through and he looked more handsome than ever. "I can feel it. It's like I'm ten pounds lighter. Can you feel it?" he asked, looking around at his people.

A cheer went up across the room as fists were raised in the air. Men clasped one another in triumphant hugs. Women broke down in joyous tears. Colin's father enveloped him in his arms and together the king and the prince laughed, overjoyed—victorious.

Paige looked at her sisters, her own heart as light as air. They had done it. The people of Tarsina were safe.

"Luka! Guards! Kindly escort my mother and her men to the dungeon!" Colin shouted, releasing his father and turning toward the broken form of the queen.

"With pleasure," Luka said, rushing forward.

The queen struggled to her feet as she was hauled up by Luka and one of his men. She glared at Colin and her husband as she was dragged by.

"You ignorant fools," she spat. "You have no idea what you've done."

Colin and the king simply stared her down, looking disgusted, disappointed, and sad. The second the queen was gone, Corinne rushed forward and threw her arms around Colin's neck. He lifted her off her feet and twirled her around as everyone in the room applauded. Finally Colin placed her back on the ground and cupped her face in his hands.

"My wife," he said, grinning down at her.

"My husband," she replied.

And then they kissed as if it was their first kiss ever. Paige cheered and applauded for the new princess along with her loyal subjects. Piper wrapped her arms around Paige and Phoebe put her head on her shoulder. They all smiled as they watched the happily-ever-after moment transpire. The magical prince had married his mortal love. It was really a fairy tale come true.

Nothing was ever going to be the same for the people of Tarsina. Everything was just getting better.

Chapter Thirteen

Paige took a deep breath and let it out slowly. She couldn't believe it was finally over. She couldn't believe she and her sisters and Leo had saved Tarsina. She couldn't believe that she was actually getting a chance to wear her wedding gown.

Turning sideways to check her reflection in the mirror, Paige knew she looked drop-dead gorgeous, and she gave herself a pleased little smile. It would have been a waste to give this dress to anyone else. After all, it had actually been *made* for her. It wouldn't have looked half as good on anyone else.

The double doors to her chamber opened and in stepped Piper and Phoebe. Piper wore a long blue gown with bell sleeves and a square neckline. Her hair was gathered up in hundreds of spiral curls that cascaded down her back. Phoebe wore a hot pink gown with a plunging neckline and a train that swished behind her as she walked. Around her neck was a gorgeous diamond choker from the royal jewel collection that Corinne had loaned to her. With the queen tapping her foot in a magically reinforced cell somewhere, Corinne had claimed control of all the royal family's precious trinkets and baubles. The first thing she had done was offer them up to her friends.

"You guys look stunning," Paige said, turning to face them.

"Oh, Paige," Piper said, looking her up and down with a wistful smile. "You would have made a beautiful bride. I'm glad you didn't, but you would have."

"Thanks," Paige said with a grin. "I just hope that white is an appropriate color for a knighting ceremony."

"Is that what's happening tonight?" Phoebe asked as she linked arms with Paige and walked back out into the hall. "Are we being knighted?"

Leo stepped away from the wall looking perfectly James Bond in a pristine tux. "I'm being knighted," he said. "You guys are becoming Ladies."

"I thought I already *was* a lady," Paige said.

"Just go with it," Piper told her as Leo took her hand.

"Whatever," Paige said. "But if we're becoming Ladies, you should probably stop calling us 'you guys,'" she suggested to Leo.

"Point taken," he said with a smirk.

Together the Halliwells swept down the huge stone staircase at the center of the castle and walked along the stone floor hallway to the ballroom. Luka and a few other guards stood outside the doors in their sentry positions. As Paige and the others approached, Luka stepped away from the wall and dropped into a low bow.

"Good evening," he said with a smile. "I have the honor of announcing you tonight."

"Announcing us?" Phoebe asked.

"Yes, miss. They're all waiting for you," Luka replied.

"They all who?" Paige asked.

"Everyone," Luka said, his eyes sparkling.

Then he turned and opened the door to the ballroom. Paige's breath escaped her as she stepped over the threshold. The cavernous room was packed to the gills with men, women, and children, all dressed to the nines. There was an even bigger crowd than there had been on the night of her first ball in Tarsina. As soon as the door opened, every last person in the room fell silent and turned to look. Paige reached out and grabbed Piper's hand. She had never seen so many people in one place in her life, and they were all staring at her.

"Your Majesties, lords, ladies, and gentlemen!" Luka called out, his voice echoing through the room. "I give you our heroes and honored guests of the evening, the Charmed

Ones, Piper Halliwell, Phoebe Halliwell, and Paige Matthews, and their Whitelighter, Leo Wyatt."

At that, the entire room exploded in cheers and applause. The noise was so deafening, Paige couldn't even hear Phoebe's words of surprise. As Leo led the way into the room, the crowd parted in front of them, forming an aisle up the middle of the checkerboard ballroom floor. The citizens of Tarsina clapped and shouted and cheered Paige and her family along as they walked on shaky knees, grinning all the way. At the end of the aisle, King Philip, Prince Colin, and Princess Corinne stood in front of their thrones. Paige smiled up at Corinne when she saw the beautiful gold tiara adorning her friend's hair. Corinne winked in return.

"Ladies and gentlemen! If I could please have your attention!" Colin shouted, his voice magically amplified to permeate the entire room. Ever so slowly the applause died down and the voices shrunk to a mere excited murmur. "We come here tonight to celebrate these brave people. People who had never been to Tarsina, who had never even heard of our kingdom and its people, but who rushed selflessly to our aid when they learned we needed their help."

Paige found herself blushing under the praise as another cheer rose up. Colin waited for the applause to die down before continuing.

"If not for their quick thinking, their bravery,

and the strength of their magic, we would not be here today," Colin said. "And so, on this night, it is our pleasure to bestow upon them the titles of Lord and Ladies of Tarsina."

As the crowd cheered again, Corinne stepped forward and took Paige's hand.

"This is where you all kneel," she whispered, glancing from Paige to her sisters and Leo.

Paige nodded and grasped Corinne's fingers as she lowered herself to her knees. It wasn't an easy action in her heavy gown, and she was grateful for her friend's help. Paige smiled at Phoebe and Piper as they all squared their shoulders and looked up at Colin. Getting this title was a serious thing, so Paige attempted to look as somber as the occasion required, but inside she was so giddy she could laugh. She was really living a fairy tale here. A king was about to bestow a title upon her in front of an entire kingdom. Even a huge, romantic wedding couldn't have been better.

The prince pulled out a gleaming silver sword and laid it across both his hands. Bowing, he handed the sword to his father, who lifted it high above his head, the point to the sky.

"I, King Philip the Third of Tarsina, do hereby bestow upon you, Paige Matthews, the title of Lady of Tarsina," he said, his voice bellowing across the room.

He smiled down at Paige and gently touched the flat side of the sword to one of her shoulders.

Then he lifted it over her head and touched it to the other. Paige bowed her head as he did this, feeling it was the proper and solemn thing to do. The king moved on to Phoebe, then Piper, then Leo, performing the same ritual on each of them.

"You can stand," Corinne whispered when the king was through. "Now turn and face the crowd."

Paige did as she was told, holding her breath as she gazed down at the hundreds upon hundreds of expectant faces. She still couldn't believe that all these people had actually turned out to see her and her family. In a strange way, it seemed as if they were finally being recognized for all the good they had done. No one in her own world might ever know about the epic battles she and her sisters waged each day, but here the people did know. And they appreciated all the sacrifice, all the hard work. The entire kingdom had come out to celebrate the Charmed Ones.

"Ladies and gentlemen!" Colin called out, stepping forward. "I give you Lord Leo Wyatt of Tarsina!"

The crowd burst into applause as Leo nodded his head at them.

"Lady Piper Halliwell of Tarsina!" Colin said. Piper grinned and flushed.

"Lady Phoebe Halliwell of Tarsina!"

Phoebe lifted a hand in a wave to acknowledge the cheers and gave a little curtsy.

"And finally, Lady Paige Matthews of Tarsina!" Colin finished.

If possible, the cheers grew even louder as Paige swept into a curtsy. These people knew what Paige had been willing to do to save them, and they wanted to show her how thankful they were. Paige's heart felt as if it was about to burst as Corinne and Colin each hugged her in turn. Somehow everything had turned out the way it should. The right people were married, the right people were ruling the kingdom, and Tarsina was at peace.

"I can't tell you how happy I am for you," Paige told Corinne and Colin as they gathered into a little huddle.

"We owe it all to you, Paige," Colin said as the band started to play and the people broke into pairs on the dance floor. "We owe it all to you."

"Paige? Paige! Are you awake?"

Piper knocked on Paige's door and then walked right in. Paige looked up at her sister from under the blankets on her bed and sighed. Piper laughed and then covered her mouth with her hand.

"Whatcha doing?" Piper asked as she stepped into the room, crossing her arms over her chest.

Paige knew she looked pathetic. She was laying flat on her back in her sweats, the sheets pulled all the way up to her chin. Hanging on the back of her closet door directly across from her bed was her almost wedding dress. For some reason, try as she might, she could not stop staring at it.

"I think I miss Tarsina," Paige said with a sigh. She picked up the string on her hooded sweatshirt and toyed with it.

"You miss getting all dressed up, huh?" Piper asked, walking over and sitting on the edge of Paige's bed.

Paige nodded slightly.

"And you miss all those servants waiting on you hand and foot, don't ya?" Piper asked.

Paige sighed again and looked up wistfully, thinking of those amazing breakfasts and the way all those people jumped whenever she moved. Sometimes it had been kind of annoying, but most of the time it had been really, really cool.

"Don't get me wrong, Piper, I'm glad to be home," Paige said, pushing herself up and leaning back on her pillows. "But I have to admit, it was kind of nice being a princess for a few days there."

"I know," Piper said, reaching over to curl a lock of Paige's hair around her finger. "That's why we've decided to reintroduce you to normal society slowly."

"What do you mean?" Paige asked, her brow wrinkling.

"Phoebe?" Piper called.

The door was kicked open and in walked

Phoebe, carrying a tray that was heaped with French toast, strawberries, coffee, and juice.

"Ta da!" Phoebe said, placing the tray in front of Paige.

"You guys! What did you do?" Paige asked, her eyes lighting up as the yummy scents made her stomach grumble.

"We just figured that having a fairy tale life dangled in front of you and then snatched away at the last second might be kind of traumatic," Phoebe said, sitting down next to Paige and curling her legs underneath her. "No matter how much you kept saying you didn't want it."

"I didn't want to be married and have a kid," Paige said, popping a strawberry into her mouth. "But the perks *were* kind of spectacular."

"Tell me about it," Phoebe said. "Did you *see* that guy I was dancing with at the ball? They don't make 'em like that in the real world."

Paige laughed and looked at her sisters. "Well, I did learn one thing from this whole experience," she said.

"Never trust the mother-in-law?" Piper suggested.

"Ooh! I know! Never send me and Leo in as spies!" Phoebe put in.

"No, no, no," Paige said with a smile. "After seeing Corinne and Colin together, I've decided that no matter what happens to me from here on out, I am not going to compromise when it comes to love."

"Oh, sweetie. You really liked him, didn't you?" Phoebe said, laying her arm across Paige's back.

"I did," Paige said with a pang in her heart. "But it was just not meant to be. That doesn't mean that there isn't someone out there for me, though. Someone I can really fall in love with. And one of these days, I'm gonna find him."

"We know you will, honey," Piper said with a smile.

Paige nodded and picked up her coffee mug with both hands. She took a long sip and closed her eyes, letting the warm liquid soothe her from the inside out.

"And, hey, if the guy I love comes with a palace and some servants," she said with a sly grin, "that'd be nice too."

About the Author

Emma Harrison is an editor-turned-writer who has written many books for the Charmed series. She lives in New Jersey with her husband.

"We all need to believe that magic exists."

–Phoebe Halliwell, "Trial by Magic"

When Phoebe Halliwell returned to San Francisco to live with her older sisters, Prue and Piper, in Halliwell Manor, she had no idea the turn her life—*all* their lives—would take. Because when Phoebe found the Book of Shadows in the Manor's attic, she learned that she and her sisters were the Charmed Ones, the most powerful witches of all time. Battling demons, warlocks, and other black-magic baddies, Piper and Phoebe lost Prue but discovered their long-lost half-Whitelighter, half-witch sister, Paige Matthews. The Power of Three was reborn.

Look for a new Charmed novel every other month!

Published by Simon & Schuster
® & © 2004 Spelling Television Inc. All Rights Reserved.

"We're the protectors of the innocent.
We're known as the Charmed Ones."

–Phoebe Halliwell, "Something Wiccan This Way Comes"

Go behind the scenes of television's sexiest supernatural thriller with *The Book of Three*, the *only* fully authorized companion to the witty, witchy world of *Charmed*!

Published by Simon & Schuster